The Missing Men
of the *Sirius*

The Missing Men
of the *Sirius*

by
Georges Price

translated, annotated and introduced by
Brian Stableford

A Black Coat Press Book

Visit our website at www.blackcoatpress.com

ISBN 978-1-61227-387-7. First Printing. April 2015. Published by Black Coat Press, an imprint of Hollywood Comics.com, LLC, P.O. Box 17270, Encino, CA 91416.
Printed in the United States of America.

Introduction

Les Trois disparus du "Sirius" by Georges Price, here translated as *The Missing Men of the Sirius*, was first published in Tours by Alfred Mame et fils in 1896.

The author, whose real name was Ferdinand-Gustave Petitpierre, was born in Nantes in 1853 and died in Paris in 1922. He wrote numerous books, beginning with *Historiettes de France et d'Espagne* [Episodes from the History of France and Spain] (1881), sticking to non-fiction until he supplied a novelette to the *roman feuilleton* slot of *La Science Illustrée* in 1895, "Les huit cents doubloons de Springfield"[1], which describes the tribulations of a brilliant naval engineer persecuted by a less talented but more powerful rival, who is finally driven to a highly unusual melodramatic confrontation.

Although he continued to write non-fiction books of various kinds thereafter, he supplemented them with a notable series of Vernian adventure stories, of which *Les Trois disparus du "Sirius"* was the first, and its sequel, *Les Chasseurs d'epaves* [The Wreck-Clearers], the second. They were followed by three other novels from the same publisher: *L'Étoile du Pacifique* [The Star of the Pacific] (1911), *La Mine d'or infernale* [The Infernal Gold-Mine] (1920) and the posthumously published *La Grotte mystérieuse* [The Mysterious Cavern] (1923).

Price came rather late to the field of Vernian romance, and in thematic terms, he added very little to it, but he did bring a considerable narrative flair and gloss

---

[1] tr. as "Springfield's Doubloons" in the Black Coat Press anthology *The Conqueror of Death*, ISBN 978-1-61227-230-6.

5

to the genre, which many of its previous contributors had lacked to some degree. The principal organ of Vernian fiction, the *Journal des Voyages*, had slipped gradually downmarket since its foundation in 1877; the feuilletons it featured were often a trifle rough-hewn, and their narrative structure often suffered from the habit that many feuilleton writers had of making up their stories as they went along while they were actually in the process of serialization. Price did not work in that way, and, of all the chroniclers of "extraordinary voyages" in the Vernian vein, he was one of the most sophisticated, in terms of his narrative method and his ability to maintain the suspense of his plots, making good use of the plot/counterplot structure so deftly deployed in *Les Trois disparus du "Sirius."*

It might be said in criticism of Price's fiction that he stretched plausibility to the utmost limit, and somewhat beyond, but that was part and parcel of the game, and could be considered the very essence of Vernian romance—and, indeed, of adventure fiction in general, which thrives on million-to-one-coincidences and hairsbreadth escapes. Like many Vernian romances, his books were aimed by their publisher primarily at younger readers, although Price would undoubtedly have considered—as Verne did of the vast majority of his own works—that there was nothing juvenile about them, either in their determined celebration of maritime heroism, or their steadfast championship of the virtue of scientific thinking and technological ingenuity.

Les Trois disparus du "Sirius" does, however, compare well with the best English "boys' books," which frequently celebrated the first of those qualities, although they were often lax in the latter respect—which is why the specifically Vernian element of French fiction of that type gives it a distinctive intellectual quality, as well as a particular flavor of sophistication.

Les Trois disparus du "Sirius" is, in essence, a pure entertainment, designed for amusement, and thus neither requires nor stands to benefit from any elaborate critical commentary; when one has said that it is a jolly good read, one has said everything necessary. Its Vernian component does add a particular didactic element to that entertainment value, however, not so much in the detail of Dr. Sergeant's bold technical improvisations—in which modern readers more familiar with the problems of contriving efficient life-support systems will be able to spot several flaws—but in the general attitude that they embody, arguing for the immense utility of knowledge and education, not merely in practical terms but in psychological terms too, as key armaments of survival in more ways than one. That was a worthwhile endeavor in 1896, and remains one today.

This translation was made from the copy of the Mame edition reproduced on the Bibliothèque Nationale's *gallica* website.

Brian Stableford

PART ONE
THE PRISONERS OF THE SEA

I

How, after a disagreeable quadrille,
a ship's lieutenant was charged
with an equally disagreeable mission

On Thursday 5 September 1892 there was a dance aboard the front-line battleship *Guichen*, carrying the flag of Vice-Admiral de la Rénolière, anchored at Piraeus with the rest of the squadron.

The French vessels had been moored in the port for a week, and following a tradition that went back to the Battle of Navarin, which profoundly unites our fatherland and Greece, our officers and matelots had been fêted all week in every possible way by the Hellenes. On the other hand, there had also been at Piraeus, at the same time, a Russian battleship, the *Dimitri-Donskoi*, and a Spanish frigate, the *Almanza*. On the day after Cronstadt,[2] the Russians had invited their French comrades to a fraternal feast, and the Spaniards, not wanting to be left out, had deployed all their Castilian amiability

---

[2] Negotiations for the Franco-Russian alliance, signed in August 1892 began in earnest when the French fleet was officially welcomed in the naval base of Kronstadt, or Cronstadt.

in their regard—to such an extent that the worthy admiral, pulled in all directions by all these assaults of refined courtesy and cordial hospitality, lacking the time to display the marks of his gratitude, had made the decision to thanks everyone at once by offering those friends of France one of those celebrations that obtain from their setting and the ingenuity of our mariners such a particular glamour and such an original flavor.

The deck of the *Guichen* had been transformed into a magnificent ballroom, covered by a tent descending over the rails, entirely lit by clusters of electric lightbulbs disposed in chandeliers made with sheaves of weapons. Electric footlights garlanded the gun-turrets, which disappeared under tangles of green plants, only allowing the polished bronze of their formidable breeches to show in the midst of that luxuriant ornamentation.

The flags of all the countries, draped by improvised and adroit interior decorators, hid the austerity of the iron walls, raised in large pleats maintained by dazzling trophies. The signal-stations had been stripped of all their signal-flags, which hid the canvas vault beneath a multicolored lining. The *Guichen*'s excellent orchestra had taken its place on the bridge, and underneath the aft canopy a comfortable and original buffet had been set up, illuminated by luminous clusters disposed behind enormous mirror-balls, which reflected the light at the whim of their immense facets, scintillating like implausibly enormous precious stones.

Had it not been for the military appearance of the buffet attendants and the martial aspect of the cannons and trophies, even hidden beneath flowers, no one would have thought that the gracious ballroom was accommodated in one of the powerful and terrible engines of death that ironclad vessels are. No one could have imagined that the polished floor, trodden by dainty satin slippers and the iridescent hall in which so many pretty dressed and brilliant uniforms were whirling in the warm radiance of Edison lamps, might someday require to be transformed into a bloody battlefield, disemboweled by shells, swept by machine-guns, and threatened by the fulgurant impact of torpedoes. No one could have imagined that, of all those flags associating the bizarreries of their bright colors, there might one day remain nothing but a shredded tricolor, proudly nailed to the sheet-metal of the masthead of war.

We ought to add that no one was thinking about those terrible possibilities. Aboard the *Guichen*, people were amusing themselves, without any afterthought or philosophical reflections, the naval officers enjoying the present movement like brave men for whom such opportunities are rare, and the guests, savoring the originality of the setting, surrendering to the charm of French hospitality. Invitations to the dance had been snatched up.

So, while the quadrilles were already beginning to find the space cramped, the launches were still bringing cargoes of bright dresses, decorated shirt-fronts and black suits to the starboard stairway, coming alongside without encumbrance, illuminated in their journey by the luminous beams of searchlights and colored flares, which, as they burst, cast an intense light over the harbor and houses of Piraeus.

The admiral, installed at the port of the gangway, escorted by the general staff of the *Guichen* and its duty officers, was greeting the guests and expending a large provision of amiable words which he had sagely stored up with that intention.

Monsieur de la Rénolière was a man of the world in every sense of the term, as perfect a gentleman as he was a mariner. Nevertheless, after a sojourn of an hour and a half at the gangway, he was seriously beginning to wish that the last guests would arrive. His entire stock of welcoming formulae was exhausted; he was making the most energetic efforts of the imagination in order not to repeat himself, and, during a moment of calm, he said to one of his officers as he put on a third pair of white gloves:

"I've already had two pairs killed under me."

To which the officer replied with a fit of hilarity conventionally adjusted to rank.

At that moment, a highly decorated individual disembarked from his launch; as soon as the admirable had seen him he took two steps forward to meet him, his arms extended. "Ah, my dear Consul," he said, amicably. "You're late."

"That's true, Admiral," the French consul replied, in a low voice, "but I've just received important news, and I confess that I'm really not in the mood to enjoy myself."

"What news?"

"I'll communicate it to you shortly, inasmuch as I have a dispatch for you. Give me a sign at the first moment of liberty you have, and we'll talk in your cabin. There's no need to disturb the party."

"But what is it? Some diplomatic complication?"

"Less and more, Admiral. There's cholera at Beyrouth."[3]

---

[3] I have retained the author's French spelling of Beyrouth rather than substituting the modern Beirut.

During that short conversation, two men were chatting while sitting in a corner formed by a gun-turret and the bulwark.

One of the two was a naval lieutenant, about twenty-eight years old. Bronzed and energetic in appearance, the young officer seemed slightly melancholy, as if out of place in the middle of the party. His companion, who was much older, was wearing a simple black suit, and not wearing any decoration. By his distinguished but rather stiff appearance, as well as the blond tint of his beard and hair, which was beginning to turn silvery at the temples, it was easy to recognize an Englishman.

That gentleman was Sir Owen J. Townsend, a distinguished naturalist, created a baronet by Her Majesty the Queen for his fine work on oceanic fauna and flora, and the owner of the magnificent steam-yacht *Investigator*, presently anchored at Piraeus. That superb pleasure-boat had attracted the admiration of our officers; it drew eight hundred tons and contained, as well as its master's luxury apartments, marvelously well-equipped laboratories, an abundantly-provided library and a complete set of instruments dedicated for the studies to which Sir Owen was devoted.

The naval lieutenant's name was Georges de Malher, and he was the English naturalist's nephew by marriage. He had, in fact, married a young woman born and brought up in France, whose father, Monsieur Aubertot, now deccased, was a French ironmaster, but whose mother was Sir Owen's sister.

In his capacity as a dedicated seaman, the scientist had acquired a considerable affection for his nephew, by reason of the latter's profession. As his yacht was cruising at present along the coast of Egypt, he had taken the opportunity offered by the French fleet's stopover at Piraeus to cross the Mediterranean and come to shake his young relative's hand, offering him a few amicable consolations at the same time.

The officer was, indeed, somewhat melancholy; he had only been married six months when he had been obliged to take command of the *Sirius*, a light vessel of barely six hundred tones, attached to the Levant squadron in order to do the work of a dispatch-boat, something akin to the work of an errand-boy. It was not that the situation was repugnant to him; after all, he was the master of his modest ship, just as the commander of the *Richelieu* was aboard his. His general staff only comprised the vessel's ensign, a midshipman first-class, a purser, a physician and a pharmacist, and his crew only consisted of thirty men, but he was able to meditate the aphorism of the conquering Roman according to whom it was better to be the first in a small village than the second in Rome.

He was, however, having difficulty reconciling himself to the separation that the unsentimental Ministry of Marine had imposed on him at the very beginning of his marriage, and he needed all his Christian resignation and all his instincts of discipline not to curse his inconvenient superior.

Thus, during the ball, Sir Owen was occupied in seriously scolding his relative for his gloomy expression, and trying to comfort him, after his fashion.

"Come on, my friend—you have scarcely three months to wait before going home. Three months will soon pass."

"That's easy for you to say..."

"Not at all. Yes, I know, you're going to tell me that I'm an old bachelor—that's perfectly true, but it doesn't prove anything. You'll see how glad you'll be to see your wife again. You'll love her a hundred times more than if you'd never left her. Believe me, although I'm a simple naturalist, I'm something of a psychologist, and I can assure you that absence is to affection what pickles are to roast beef. Forgive me that ludicrous comparison, but it renders my thought accurately."

To which Georges de Malher replied: "All that's charming, but I can assure you that I'd give three years' advancement right now, and many other things besides, including the portfolio of my ministry, to be in the little white house hidden under tall trees at Mourillon, in which my wife is probably playing chess with a respectable female cousin.

At that moment, a frigate captain deigned to ask Georges to make up a foursome with him. One cannot do otherwise than be very flattered by such a request from a superior. The young officer bowed, took his place in a quadrille with some dancing-partner or other, muddled up the steps, endured the irritated gaze of the frigate captain and his uncle's ironic smiles, and, having escorted his partner back to her seat, experienced the first moment of real satisfaction that he had known for a long time.

As he was returning to Sir Owen, an officer with shoulder-knots approached him and took him to one side.

"Monsieur," he said "the Admiral requests that you come to speak to him immediately, without telling anyone. Please come with me."

Very surprised, Georges bowed. He followed his guide through the crowd of guests, went into the aft apartments, went through a door guarded by a matelot armed with a halberd, and waited while the orderly officer went to inform the Admiral.

Monsieur de la Rénolière, very worried, was alone with the French consul

"My dear Monsieur de Malher," he said, "I summoned you immediately because the mission I have to give you will not suffer any delay. You're to go back aboard the *Sirius* immediately, light the fires, and as soon as you're under pressure, you're to go to the quay to collect a cargo. Cholera has broken out in Beyrouth with great violence. Our nationals, and the schools that we protect, are being decimated. In sum, given our role in the Orient, we must go immediately to the aid of the unfortunate populations tested by the scourge.

"Monsieur le Consul has taken urgent measures this evening to have medicines prepared, and all the disinfectant that you can carry. As soon as you're moored, you'll take aboard six physicians, two of them civilian, chosen by Monsieur le Consul, and four belonging to our sanitary service. You'll go directly to Beyrouth and await orders there, while reconciling, in accordance with your conscience, the cares of your crew and the duties of humanity."

"Understood, Admiral. I'll leave immediately."

"Go, Monsieur—I'm counting on your discretion. There will be time for people to hear the sad news tomorrow. The mission is not without danger; I wish you good luck."

Five minutes later, Georges de Malher took his leave of Sir Owen, who asked for explanations in vain.

"I'll give them to you aboard the *Sirius*, my dear uncle, if you would like me to give you hospitality until tomorrow. If not, I'm bound to silence."

"So be it," said Sir Owen. And he descended into the launch in company with the young man, not without having phlegmatically lit a cigar.

II

In which we make the acquaintance
of Jean Halgouët, alias Quosé

While the elegant crowd was packed on the deck of the *Guichen*, ten French matelots belonging to the crew of the *Sirius* were having a party of their own on shore in the company of three Russians mariners and four Spanish comrades.

The French sailors did not speak a word of Russian or Spanish, the Russians did not understand Spanish or French, and the Spaniards did not have the slightest idea of French or Russian, but that did not prevent the joyful troop from getting along very well and pooling their roubles, douros and hundred-sou pieces during varied and repeated ports of call in taverns.

The leader of the band was a Breton matelot named Jean Halgouët, "born a native of Billiers, near Muzillac, two steps from Questembert in Morbihan." That was how he had explained his civil estate to the Russians, who had saluted admiringly, and the Spaniards who had bowed with dignity.

The said Jean Halgouët was tanned like Cordovan leather, having already spent, as he also said, "eight years of navigation between the timbers." He was of medium height, but as agile and muscular as an acrobat. Passionately fond of the sea, glimpsing nothing beyond the horizon of his life but a fishing-boat and nets when he retired from the navy, he might have earned promotion if his imagination had not led him astray. Under the pretext that the land is made for amusement, he indulged when in port in a series of distractions that had often provoked complaints from the narrow-minded indigenes he had honored with his pranks—with the consequence that, in spite of his real intelligence, his qualities as a mariner and his curious education, he had remained a simple second-class matelot.

We mentioned his curious education. In fact, Jean Halgouët had had as a master an old long-haul captain retired to Billiers, who belonged to a rather rare breed of mariner: the mariner smitten with the classics, a translator of Horace and reader of Homer. The worthy captain, struck by the intelligence of his young neighbor, had undertaken his education, and the result of his lessons had been singular. Jean was somewhat hit-and-miss in orthography, but he knew mythology thoroughly. He only had a vague idea of the history of the discovery of America, but he could have recounted from memory, without any error, the expedition of the Argonauts— "fine matelots, even though they were manning an old clog." He firmly believed, if by chance he gave the matter any thought, that Louis XII had been the successor of Louis XI, but he was perfectly certain about the role of Neptune as the god of the sea, and had even retained the habit of employing as an oath the undignified *quos ego* that Virgil had put into the god's mouth.[4] Thus, his comrades had nicknamed him Quosego, and by abbreviation, Quosé—on hearing which, the Spaniards had immediately stated calling him Don José.

---

[4] This phrase, uttered by Neptune in the *Aeneid* while threatening the winds, was widely adopted as an admonition to naughty children, although its literal translation—Whom I—makes no sense at all.

Furthermore, Jean Halgouët was a convinced patriot, and, as a good Breton matelot, nurtured a hatred of the English. Every time he found himself in the presence of one of those "hereditary enemies," he strove to play some prank on him, after his fashion, and it often happened that those amiable practical jokes concluded in boxing matches, in which the islanders rarely came out on top. Quosé had a particular manner of bringing the heel of his boot into the contest that amazed the English, accustomed to classical boxing, and gave them, by courtesy of a consecutive and obligatory week's rest, all the leisure required to meditate on the superiority of French kick-boxing.

It was that that a year before, finding himself in a tavern in Cavite in the Philippines, he had picked a quarrel with a Scottish sailor of gigantic stature, on whom he had played the little joke moving his glass of *aguardiente* with the tip of a cane he was holding. The Scotsman had bounded over the table and had begun raining a formidable hail of punches on the Breton's hard skull, but the latter, without getting excited, had taken hold of both sides of the collar of his adversary's jacket, and had swiftly turned them inside-out while pulling the garment down along the body, which had had the effect of binding both the giant's arms—after which he had coiffed him with a enormous honey-pot that happened to come to hand, crying: *Sic vos non vobis mellificatis, apes!*[5]

---

[5] *Sic vos non vobis* [Thus you do, but not for yourselves] were the first four words of a set of verses left deliberately unfinished by Virgil. Quosé's version is addressed to the bees [*apes*] that made the honey in the pot [*mellificatis*].

Comrades had intervened on both sides; the Spanish police, who, by some miracle, were not far away, had got involved, and the affair had not had any further consequences—but the furious Scotsman had sworn to avenge himself on Quosé in particular and the French in general, which had made the Breton laugh.

That evening, Quosé, desiring to do honor to the Russians and the Spaniards, had put his imagination to work. He was, moreover, quite tranquil, all the police in Piraeus being on the docks in order honor to the guests of the French squadron and to help with the fireworks. Thus, he was parading through the streets a large manikin made of two poles in the form of a cross, covered with a reefer-jacket and coiffed with a beret, which he was presenting to the first-floor windows and knocking on the panes—which provoked the appearance of frightened heads protected by strange nightcaps. He knocked on the door of an unfortunate money-changer, from whom he gravely requested a drachma in change, offering politely to pay the commission, and bought candles from a grocer with which he lit up the shop-front of the pork-butcher Epaminondas Zoopoulos, who thought it was a fire and roused the entire neighborhood.

We must agree that, viewed objectively, Quosé's jokes ought to have been impregnated with a little more attic salt, but such as they were, I admit, they had the gift of amusing the band greatly—which, before going back to the ships, went cheerfully into the establishment of the widow Dracon Basili, who had a raki shop in the Place Philopoemen that was highly reputed among sailors of different nationalities.

A group of drinkers was already there: five or six fair-haired men, vigorous and red-faced, wearing at breast height, embroidered in red on their blue jerseys, the name of the English yacht *Investigator*.

Jean Halgouët's companions did not pay any attention at first to those customers, and occupied themselves conscientiously with the confection of a formidable punch, destined simultaneously to cement a friendship that was already at least two hours old, and to soften the bitterness of a separation that would probably be eternal.

At the moment when the liquor began to burn, one of the Frenchmen observed to Halgouët that the Englishmen seemed to be affording them a very particular attention. Indeed, the mariners of the *Investigator* were whispering, their eyes fixed on the band, and one of them, whose back had been turned, had swiveled on his bench and was directing a stare charged with anger at Halgouët himself.

On his companion's remark, the Breton ceased momentarily stirring the punch with his ladle, and examined the Englishmen.

"Well, well," he said, "there's a funny coincidence. You see that big fellow looking at me as if his eyes were Hotchkiss guns? Well, that's my Englishman from Cavite in the Philippines—the one who consumed, without wishing to, such a large quantity of the honey of the gentle bees of Hymetta."

"Impossible!"

"The very same. Hey, you over there, the man with the red beard, one might think that you recognize me?"

"Yes, I recognize you perfectly."

"Good! In that case, old chap, you'll give me the pleasure of leaving us tranquil and telling the gentle lambs accompanying you not to pay any further attention to us."

The Englishman got up, advanced into the middle of the room, folded his arms and said: "Would you care to give me a return match?"

"No, old chap, no—for two reasons. The first is that I can't insult these Messieurs by neglecting the punch that they've confided to my care, and the second is that it's late and we have to go back aboard. So, if you please, let's leave it until another time."

And, still calm, the Breton drew out some flaming punch, and let it fall back in a blue spray. The other Englishmen, standing up, had gathered behind the man from Cavite.

"All right," replied the latter, coolly. "We'll leave it for another time, but I can tell you, as true as my name's Thomas Tingle, that you're a coward, like all Frenchmen."

At that word, there was a frightful bacchanal. The Frenchmen had bounded to their feet, and the punch-bowl spilled. The Spaniards and the Russians, who had not understood what was said, but who could see that their friends had a quarrel, did likewise. The Englishmen advanced, fists clenched. A brawl was imminent.

Halgouët did not lose his head. He grasped the gravity of the situation immediately. He threw himself in front of his friends and stopped them with a gesture.

"One moment," he said. "It's a personal matter between this parishioner and me, and I don't want anyone else to get mixed up in it. As for you, my son, I understand that you have a grudge against me, although I've only given you sweeteners. But as I don't have a grudge against you, I don't have the slightest desire to fight you—except that, as you've just insulted me, I propose a wager. You have a red beard? Well, I'll wager three francs two sous—what you call half a crown—that within a minute, I can tint your beard bright blond. It's agreed, of course, that no one else mixes in with it?"

The Englishman sniggered, and put himself on guard. "Agreed. Are we ready? Attention! One, two, three..."

Quosé advanced toward the Englishman in a very correct boxing stance. Everyone wondered what he was going to do and how he was going to carry out the tinting operation, which appeared to be passably complicated.

The answer was not long in coming.

The Breton began by launching a couple of punches at his opponent; then, when the latter riposted, and without worrying about his punches, he swiftly crouched down, flattening himself on the ground, so to speak, grabbed hold of the giant's ankles with his muscular arms, lifted him off the ground, carried him away, gesticulating, and plunged him head first into an immense bin full of golden yellow flour, where the unfortunate remained planted for a second or two shoulder-deep. While the Englishmen ran forward to help their comrade, Jean Halgouët threw some coins on to the table before the bewildered eyes of Madame Dracon Basili, and went out, accompanied by his entire troop, who were writhing with laughter. And while they could still hear the imprecations of the British sailors, they rapidly went across the Place Philopoemen and took the shortest route back to the harbor, where the launch was stationed for the men who had leave until midnight. The Frenchmen took their leave, with forceful handshakes, of the Russians and the Spaniards, delighted with such a pleasant evening and its final episode, and headed for the spot where the boat ought to be waiting.

To their great astonishment, it was no longer there, but they found in its stead one of their comrades, who informed them that the *Sirius* was maneuvering to come abreast of the quay, where it was to take on a mysterious cargo and depart for an unknown destination.

An hour later, Jean Halgouët, alias Quosé, and his companions rejoined the vessel.

In the meantime, the Englishmen freed Thomas Tingle from the disagreeable situation in which the Breton had left him. Coated to the waist in maize flour, the sailor, who had it in his eyes, his nose and his mouth, was coughing, sneezing, swearing and swallowing, in order to pull himself together, strong doses of raki. At the same time, he dusted his red beard, which, in accordance with his promise, Quosé had tinted flaxen blond with the accursed flour. When he had completely recovered, he nearly suffered a congestion on taking a exact account of the further humiliation that his adversary had just inflicted on him.

"Listen to me," he said to his companions. "If ever I have the chance to sink the *Sirius* and drown every accused Frenchman aboard her, I swear on my beard, red or blond, that I won't miss out on it."

The next day, Thomas Tingle learned that Sir Owen Townsend had given the order to make everything ready to sail, and that the *Investigator* would be traveling in convoy with the *Sirius*.

III
We're Sinking!

The French consul took his leave of Monsieur de la
Rénolière immediately after Georges' departure and returned to shore in the company of a naval physician immediately designated by the Admiral to direct the mission and to supervise the preparations. Under their energetic direction, a part of the cargo that the *Sirius* was to
take aboard was brought to the quay by first light. Immediately informed, the depots of chemical products
were able to expedite from Athens, by the first train
leaving for Piraeus, a number of barrels of various disinfectants, which were continually followed by other con-
signments. At the same time, the pharmacists of the Rue
d'Hermes put together crates of medicines, urgently requisitioned, which, as soon as the last nail was driven in,
took the same route as the disinfectants, accompanied by
several alcohol-fueled stills destined to furnish purified
water at all points where the water-supply seemed doubtful, as well as bales of rubber-coated fabric to prevent
the contamination of bedding.

Physician-Major Lucien Sergeant, appointed as
head of the medical mission by Monsieur de la
Rénolière, supervised the organization of this precious
merchandise, and found the time, while carrying out his
duty and keeping an eye on everything, to devote himself to a task that was dear to his heart.

The worthy physician had dedicated all his leisure
time for years to the study of cholera. Now, by a fatality
that he willingly attributed to bad luck, he had never—

literally never—been able to witness a cholera epidemic. Every time the terrible malady had broken out in one place, the excellent doctor had been embarked in a diametrically opposite direction. On the other hand, he had seen yellow fever at close range a hundred times over—but yellow fever did not interest him much. One has one's petty preferences.

One day he had thought that he had finally been favored by destiny; he had left San Francisco to go to Yokohama, then devastated by what was said to be a superb epidemic—but the Devil had stuck his oar in, and by the time he arrived the scourge was over.

What annoyed him was that, by reason of this perseverance in occupying himself with cholera and the innumerable communications he had sent on that subject to scientific bodies, a certain number of colleagues had become jealous of him, and had no hesitation in shrugging their shoulders at his conclusions, saying: "Sergeant? Give us a rest—he's a competent physician, but he's never seen a cholera epidemic."

Well, he was about to see one and seriously, not in the fashion of the princes of science who went to spend a couple of days in infected localities and came back with a fine report, but as a practitioner doubling as an observer, resolved to stay in the breach until the end, experimenting, studying, analyzing and, to cap it all, saving as many people as possible.

With a view to his experiments, Dr. Sergeant had thus added to the general cargo of the *Sirius* a small particular cargo, comprising everything that he needed to organize a laboratory of microbiological studies. And, to complete his joy, interrupting himself from time to time to rub his hands, he carefully checked in person the packaging of conical and round-bottomed flasks, matrasses, heat-resistant earthenware vessels, test-tubes and microscopes, and went below decks to supervise the installation of those fragile packages in the holds of the *Sirius*, where he had found a redoubt presenting all the necessary guarantees, next to the partition of the steward's stores.

The preceding observations permit an accurate judgment of Dr. Sergeant's character. Its principal feature was tenacity. To that quality he joined a perfect composure, although it was often hidden beneath an exuberance worthy of a southerner. Physically, he was a man of rather tall, quite slender stature, having retained at the age of forty-six all his scarcely-graying hair and two intact rows of very white teeth. His side-whiskers, slightly grayer than his hair but correctly trimmed into two tufts, and his slightly tanned complexion, revealed a seaman even in civilian dress. In sum, Dr. Sergeant was a worthy man, a scientist of merit, and, apart from the petty professional jealousies to which we have alluded, he only had friends.

During the loading, an operation for which, in view of the urgency, a detachment of mariners provided by other ships in the squadron was lending its assistance to the crew of the *Sirius*, the doctor walked along the quay with Commandant de Malher, frequently interrupting their conversation—for which the epidemic at Beyrouth naturally supplied the topic—to send messengers in search of a few further objects, whose description and nomenclature he scribbled on pages torn out of his notebook, at the behest of inspirations that were continually suggested to him by his thoughts, always focused on the same objective.

From time to time, other officers went over the gangplank thrown between the quay and the vessel to examine the details of the preparations. Then they returned to the shore to make sure that the various categories of merchandise were not confused, which would have complicated and prolonged the labor.

At four o'clock in the afternoon, they had almost finished the loading. The physician and Georges de Malher went back to the quay to make sure that nothing had been left out, and found themselves face to face with Sir Owen.

"Well," said the naturalist, "is everything ready?"

"It soon will be?"

"And when will you be putting to sea?"

"I'm going aboard the *Guichen* immediately to salute the Admiral and receive his final instructions. I think we'll be setting forth tomorrow morning. As I doubtless won't see you again before then, my dear uncle, I'd like to charge you with a few commissions and two or three letters for my family. One never knows who will live and who will die, does one? And as I'm going to a place where, it seems, there's a serious risk of death, I'd like..."

"Damn!" said Sir Owen. "I'd like nothing better than to accept that funereal mission, but there's one small difficulty."

"What's that, Uncle?"

"It's that I'm leaving with you, or at least at the same time as you."

"Bound for where?"

"For Beyrouth, of course. I've reflected, my dear friend, that it's my duty as an Englishman not to let the French confront danger alone. We too have compatriots in Syria damn it, so I've had my yacht loaded with all the medicines and preservatives I can get...not much, in parentheses, for you've taken almost everything. I've made everything ready to sail. Strictly speaking, I could go on ahead of you, but as it's you from whom I received the indication, I thought it more appropriate to accompany you, so..."

"So what?"

"The *Investigator* can sail in convoy with the *Sirius*, if it won't inconvenience you."

"Seriously? You've reflected that you're going to expose yourself to danger unnecessarily, without any duty obliging you to do so? You've thought about the consequences—the quarantines and all the annoyances that, even in the absence of misfortune, you might and will be subjected? You've thought about your men, whom you might perhaps be taking to their death?"

"I've thought of everything. For myself, I'm only doing what my conscience requires. As regards my men, I've informed them of the objective of the voyage, broken all engagements and told them that I'll give double pay to those who stay with me and an indemnity to those who quit. Three out of twenty-two have left. The others are acting of their own free will, so I'm morally tranquil.

"Well, my dear Uncle," said Georges, "that's very good, you know, what's you're doing."

"In truth, my dear friend, I'm not in the least afraid. Then again, I'm not married. If one of us falls ill, the other will care for him."

"We won't fall ill," interjected the doctor, who was listening to the conversation. "We're going to see a fine epidemic, and we'll save a lot of lives. Personally, I understand perfectly why Monsieur wants to see that."

Only then did Georges realize, by virtue of Sir Owen's slightly peeved expression, that he had neglected the formality of an introduction. He hastened to repair that omission, and the Englishman exchanged a vigorous handshake with the physician—the cordial handshake of men who have learned to hold one another in esteem in two minutes.

"That's good, Messieurs, let's go," said George de Malher. "We'll meet again in Beyrouth, Uncle, and we'll all do our best, you in the name of England, me in the name of France.

"And me," said the physician," in the name of humanity."

The next morning, at daybreak, the *Sirius* and the *Investigator* left the harbor and, three cables apart, set a course south-eastwards.

The *Sirius*, as we have said, was a light vessel of six hundred tons, constructed specifically with a view to speed, so her forms had all been designed to attain that end. Entirely constructed in steel, she measured forty-two meters from stem to stern, and only seven meters abeam. Her prow cleaved the water in a rigorously perpendicular line, and her flanks tapered forwards in a curve giving in cross-section, an angle as acute as an arrow-head. Her engine, of five hundred horsepower, was a veritable piece clockwork, emerged from the workshops of Indret, and activated a single propeller. The ship, thus conditioned, achieved a cruising speed of seventeen knots.

She was divided longitudinally into seven watertight compartments, communicating by means of doors whose joints, fitted with compressed rubber, were similarly impermeable to water. Every compartment was pierced in its upper section by a hatchway closed by two battens, with the same system as the doors. In case of damage or leakage, therefore, each afflicted compartment could be completely isolated, ensuring that even if it filled up, the ship could remain afloat.

The *Sirius* was fitted out as a three-masted schooner, and carried very summary artillery, composed of only six repeating cannons.

The *Investigator* had more considerable dimensions, since she gauged eight hundred tons. Constructed in iron, she had been designed in order to make use of sail or steam at will. She was therefore fitted out as a three-masted barque—which is to say that the two forward masts had square sails and only the mizzen-mast bore a brigantine. Nevertheless, her bowsprit was rudimentary and her prow affected almost the same form as that of the *Sirius*. We have already mentioned her interior fitments, very comfortable and completed by the laboratories of the natural scientist who was her owner.

These details are necessary for an understanding of what is to follow.

The *Sirius* was an incomparably better mover than the *Investigator*, which belonged to the category of mixed vessels. Thus, she would obviously obtain a rapid lead over her traveling companion, all the more so because, by reason of the urgency of her mission, her commandant had to set aside politeness and try, without worrying about outdistancing her "convoy," to arrive as rapidly as possible at her destination. Sir Owen was well aware of that situation, so he had given orders to obtain maximum speed from her engine and to stoke up the fires. Even so, he would certainly have fallen a long way behind had it not been for a brisk north-westerly breeze, which permitted him to deploy his full sail and, thus aided, to keep up with the *Sirius*.

They departed on the seventh of September at four a.m. The first phase of the journey passed without any hitch for either vessel. The sea was choppy and the sky cloudy. Nevertheless, at midday, a gap in the clouds permitted a bearing to be taken. The *Sirius* was then at 36° 29′ north latitude and 23° 32′ east longitude.

Georges de Malher went down to lunch and then, the meal having been rapidly expedited, went back up on deck in company with Dr. Sergeant. They both chatted briefly with the officer of the watch, after which, in the company of the purser, they went down to the fore holds to examine the stowage of the cargo. In the haste of the embarkation, in fact, insufficient precaution had been taken and if the sea became rough there was a possibility that the cargo might be displaced, thus harming the stability of the ship. Georges would have been able to yield his place to one of his officers, but he was in the habit of seeing to everything himself, and in any case, he had every confidence in the officer of the watch, whom he had known for a long time.

The three officers had brought a matelot with them, who was none other than our friend Jean Halgouët, alias Quosé, who was carrying a lantern. They went successively into two of the watertight compartments. When they arrived in the second, Georges noticed that a certain number of barrels had not been sufficiently secured, and might break free under the shock of the waves. The danger was imminent, and it was already perceptible that the stack of barrels, under the influence of the swell, was stirring, preliminary to a possible collapse.

As there was no way to reconstruct the basic formation of the barrels—which contained lime—while at sea, they decided to consolidate it with cables, and the purser went back up to the deck to fetch two or three men and the necessary hawsers.

As he disappeared at the top of the iron ladder to the hatchway, he crossed paths with a midshipman who was starting down.

The latter approached the lieutenant and said: "Commandant, the officer of the watch sent me to tell you about a rather singular phenomenon of these parts in the present season. The wind had just suddenly risen in the west and enveloped us in two minutes with a dense mist. One can't see the mizzen mast from the bridge. He's reducing speed immediately and sent me to inform you."

"Well," said Monsieur de Malher, "that is indeed rare. He's done well to slow down, but tell him to stop completely, sound the siren, ring the bell and ignite the position-lights."

"The position-lights are already lit."

"Good. There's no peril for the moment. I'll come up momentarily, as soon as the stack of barrels is consolidated."

The midshipman withdrew.

Scarcely two minutes had gone by when Georges, becoming impatient, said: "After all, the purser is perfectly well able to see to the securing of the cargo. This mist worries me. Let's go back up, my dear doctor."

"If you don't mind, Commandant, I'll stay. I have a quantity of instruments here necessary to my observations, and if one or two barrels were to fall on to the flasks, it would be disastrous…not for the barrels."

"So be it," said Georges. "Until later."

He started to climb in iron ladder, and was about to seize the rope hanging down from the hatchway when a mighty shock suddenly shook the *Sirius*, making her shiver in her every fiber, throwing the commandant off the top of the ladder and knocking the doctor down. At the same time, the stack of barrels collapsed; one of them hit the doctor on the head and stunned him, while Georges, unconscious, lay beside him.

Jean Halgouët, who, thanks to his simian agility, had been able to leap to one side and had emerged unscathed from the adventure, raced to the stairway, mounted the first few steps and shouted: "Help! The Commandant is injured!" Then he returned immediately to the two officers, disengaged them from the debris that was covering them, put his arms around the commandant's body, and started climbing the steps, carrying his burden. When he arrived at the hatchway, which had been open a moment before, he bumped his head.

"Eh! Quoségo!" he exclaimed. "That's a poor joke! Hey, out there, open up, damn it!"

While shouting with all the force of his lungs, he supported the unconscious officer with one arm, and his free hand struck the hermetically sealed hatch with blows of his fist.

No one came.

He perceived a distant racket outside, muffled by distance and the partitions, which caused him some anxiety.

"A thousand devils!" he said to himself. "The ship must have been hit."

"As he could not remain like that at the top of the ladder with Monsieur de Malher under his arm, waiting for help, and as he was beginning to get weary in spite of his vigor, he went back down, with the intention of lying the commandant on the floor and going back up to force the door. He laid Georges down, with his head supported on a hastily rolled-up tarpaulin, and prepared to climb up.

At that moment, however the ship oscillated; the floor of the hold lost its horizontality, and became ever closer to the vertical. The barrels were rolling around frightfully, piling up on top of one another, and Halgouët, hanging on by his heels, like an acrobat, to the iron conduit of a pump, holding each of the two bodies in one hand in order to prevent them sliding down the floor, which was now almost sheer, cried, in a tone in which his natural bravery was extinguished: "We're sinking! We're sinking!"

IV
The Collision

This is what had happened:

Aboard the *Investigator*, as we have seen, Sir Owen had tried to match his speed to that of the *Sirius*, and had succeeded, thanks to the north-westerly breeze. But he had not done so without difficulty. The attitude that suited his yacht best was that of being aslant to the wind, and for some time he had been obliged to sail with the wind behind him, which had caused him to lost impetus because part of his sail was masked by the rest.

Our Englishman was not, however, a man inclined to bow down even before natural obstacles. He was going to Beyrouth guided by two seemingly contradictory motives, but which he reconciled very logically. The first was that he did not want to be separated from his nephew, the second that he did not want a Frenchman, even if it was his nephew, to have the sole merit of hurling himself into danger, to the detriment of England. Those two excellent reasons had passed within him into the state of an obsession, and, to anyone looking into the depths of his conscience, it would not have been certain that the order in which we have listed them might not have been the wrong way round.

In those conditions he was determined to arrive at Beyrouth neither before nor after, but at the same time as the *Sirius*.

Now, Sir Owen was the absolute master of his vessel. He was, in fact, not only the owner of the *Investigator*, but also her captain. When he had had the idea of devoting his large fortune to the various studies that the ocean offered, and had, with that intention, chartered his first yacht, he had hired a captain. Then he had perceived that the presence of that intermediary, between him and his crew, singularly inconvenienced the independence of his character. So he had set to work, and as he already possessed a superior scientific education, and those very complete notions were supported by four years' experience of navigation, he had passed the examinations necessary to be able to take command of his vessel himself. Aboard the *Investigator*, he was, therefore "the master after God," and only had to account for his actions to his conscience.

By virtue of that power, as the *Sirius* drew ahead of him during the first phase of their journey, he had the fires stoked up, and as, in spite of everything, in spite of the studding-sails from the topgallants to the royals, in spite of all the stay-sails and the immense spinnaker hoisted between the mainmast and the mizzen-mast, he was still losing ground, being confident in the strength of his boilers, he had blocked the valves.

Under the influence of the superheated steam and the intense pressure, the yacht vibrated like a violin. The first mate, a former long-haul captain answering to the name of Chanticleer, who was nevertheless resolute, was alarmed by that, and could scarcely dissimulate his anxiety beneath the bearded and surly mask of a British mariner. Thanks to that stubborn recklessness, Sir Owen's ship had almost managed to keep up with the *Sirius*, but he could not continue to navigate in such conditions for long, and the engineers were anticipating the moment when the boilers would explode when, fortunately, in order to tack around the islands of the Archipelago, they were obliged to change direction. At an angle to the wind, the *Investigator* was finally able to add the full power of her fine sail to that of her engine, and, finally reassured, the engineers opened the valves.

For about an hour, the yacht had been following the *Sirius* effortlessly when the wind suddenly veered to the west. At the same time, low cloud, which had gathered to starboard, suddenly started falling toward the sea. It was seen to sink slowly down, shaving the crests of the waves, spreading out and drowning in fog the two or three fishing-boats with triangular sails that were drawing their nets over the littorals of the islands.

In a very short time the mist engulfed the *Investigator* and then masked the *Sirius*, which soon no longer appeared, in the dense vapor as anything more than a barely-sketched silhouette, and ended up disappearing altogether.

By a curious effect of the rarefaction of the droplets of water at a certain height, one could perceive distinctly, much further away than the *Sirius*, the summit of the cone of a small volcanic island, Syrtos, which, according to local tradition, had been subjected thousands of years ago to a fate analogous to that which the still-tormented sea-bed of the archipelago had reserved in our own day for the island of Santorini.

Sir Owen immediately took the same precautions that Georges de Malher had indicated on his own part. He began by sounding the siren and ringing the bell. At the same time he slowed down, ignited his positional lights, the glare of which was able to pierce the fog, posted a man at the back end of the bowsprit, and ordered the sails lowered.

On the other hand, he spotted that the helm, located on the bridge, was manned by a novice, and demanded that an experienced sailor take his place.

The replacement who presented himself was Thomas Tingle, the old enemy of the French in general and Jean Halgouët in particular. Tingle, a man sure of himself, established himself squarely on his two big feet and seized the wheel in his two solid fists.

"Pay close attention," Sir Owen said to Tingle. "The *Sirius* was two hundred and fifty yards to port of the *Investigator* a little while ago, and a little ahead. I know you don't like the French, but that's no reason to ram her. You're a good mariner. Keep watch, and move the helm a quarter westwards, where there's no land. We'll make up the lost time later."

"Don't worry, your honor," replied Thomas Tingle, without his physiognomy indicating anything but passive obedience. "I'll be careful."

At that moment, the siren and bell of the *Sirius* were heard distinctly, to port; she seemed to be getting closer. The sounds of the siren and bell of the *Sirius* became louder, and became confused with the howl of the *Investigator*'s siren and the clanging of her bell.

"They're coming toward us!" exclaimed Sir Owen. "They're going to hit us! Steer full to starboard!"

Again the sailor turned the wheel—but he turned hard to port.

"Wretch!" cried Sir Owen. "Murderer!"

He leapt upon Tingle, tore him away from the helm, and threw him down the steps of the bridge. He seized the helm with his fists, and, at the same time, put his mouth to the orifice of the loud-hailer, shouting—or rather howling—to the engine-room: "Reverse engine!"

But it was too late. A growing shadow had appeared before the yacht, and in spite of the captain's energetic spin of the wheel, in spite of the desperate intervention of the engineer, the sharp and trenchant prow of the *In-vestigator* penetrated the flank of the *Sirius* like a chisel.

The impact was terrible. Two sailors leaning over the steps of the main topsail were thrown into the sea. The first mate, who was supervising the maneuvering of the sails, raced to the bridge.

"We've been rammed!" he shouted.

"No," replied Sir Owen, "We're the ones who've done the ramming. Have Seaman Thomas Tingle put in irons, and let's take stock."

Rendered desperate at the terrible accident that the *Investigator* had just caused, and full of rage against the malefactor who had caused it, Sir Owen nevertheless conserved a cool head. On his orders, Chanticleer took his place on the bridge and the entire crew, abandoning the half-furled sails, some of which were flapping in the breeze, occupied himself in putting the boats to sea. At the same time, under the influenced of her propeller, spinning in reverse, the yacht disengaged from the *Sirius* and retreated a few brasses.

Standing under the foremast, clinging to the halyard of the jib, Sir Owen could see, five meters away, the enormous two-meter-wide vertical rip in the flank of the *Sirius*, prolonged below the water-line, that the Investi-gator's prow had made.

In a matter of seconds, the bow of the ship plunged under water, and the effect of the immersion of the ante-rior part of the vessel, displacing her center of gravity, caused her to rotate around her transversal axis, so far and so rapidly that the *Sirius* was soon in a vertical posi-tion, her stern entirely out of the water. At the same time, the sea flooded the engine room and extinguished the fires. There was a frightful rush of steam, with a dull hiss, through all the openings. So prompt had the catastrophe been that the *Sirius* had not had time to put her boats to sea. The confusion was complete.

In vain, the ensign of the watch, clinging to the handrail of the bridge and animated by the admirable sentiment of duty so profoundly anchored in the hearts of our naval officers, shouted himself hoarse, without any concern for his personal peril, howling orders to organize the abandonment of the ship; panic reigned. Some strove to operate the hawsers of the davits, but, confronted by the impossibility of outing a single boat to sea, left the launches hanging down, nose to the waves, from their lifting tackle in order to climb up toward the stern, hanging on to the ropes and the rails.

Others, acting on their own initiative, thinking that the ship might not be irredeemably lost, rapidly closed the bolts of the watertight compartments—and it was in consequence of that terrible inspiration that Georges de Malher, Dr. Sergeant and the matelot Halgouët had been imprisoned in the compartment where they were, the majority of the men being unaware that they were visiting the holds at the time.

The officer of the watch knew that. In the midst of the disarray he immediately dispatched a midshipman—the same one who had gone five minutes earlier to tell the commandant that the mist was rising. The young officer, overwhelmed, raced toward the hatchway on the deck. He had to fray a passage though the panicked comings and goings. Then, as the ship oscillated, he lost his balance, and fell against a capstan.

He got up again, and finally reached the opening that gave access to the lower deck. Already he could see the double iron door of the inferior compartment. Already he could hear the furious blows that Halgouët was striking inside his prison. But he had lost time in spite of

41

his best intentions, and the water was a meter from the hatch.

The brave young man did not hesitate. He let himself slide down the ladder. He got his hand to the bolt and was about to open it—but at that moment the vessel reared up, and the water, in a formidable rush, flooded through the opening to the deck.

The midshipman died, a victim of duty and devotion.

The *Sirius* continued to sink, relatively slowly. But the *Investigator*'s launches were within range, the sea was covered with lifebuoys, and Sir Owen had everything thrown into the water that might sustain a man. At the same time, by a providential hazard, the cloud of fog whose brief presence had been sufficient to destroy a beautiful ship and compromise so many lives gradually dissipated, and it became possible to measure the extent of the disaster and strive to restrict it.

The crewmen of the *Sirius* were grouped at the stern, and, seeing help coming, recovered their composure. The *Investigator*'s boats approached. The ensign, gnawing his fists at the idea that his commandant was dead, decided to die himself on the bridge, which the swell was beginning to reach, clinging to the binnacle and still shouting orders.

"Let the cables hang down! Let yourselves down into the water and hang on to the buoys and the chicken-cages. You'll be picked up!"

The men dropped in clusters, and soon found refuge in the *Investigator*'s boats, which courageously advanced all the way to the menacing poop of the *Sirius*, at the risk of being crushed if she tilted again, or dragged down by the eddies of its immersion. The majority of the sailors were only thinking of their own salvation, but a few thought about the heroic officer who, clinging to his post, was still occupied with saving them, stubbornly awaiting death. A quartermaster and a matelot, who were the last to remain, shouted at him: "Come on! Come on! Everyone's safe—we're waiting for you!"

"No," replied the officer.

And with his extended finger, he indicated the fore of the ship, where his commandant, two officers and a mariner had found death.

Then the quartermaster and the matelot, without any collusion other than a glance, let themselves down the ropes they were already holding. They slid down as far as the half-drowned bridge, grabbed the officer around the body, threw themselves into the water with him, and sustained him by force all the way to the *Investigator*'s launch, which picked all three of them up.

It was just in time; the *Sirius* plunged abruptly; her location was briefly marked by a temporary eddy; then the sea became tranquil again, and, but for the thousand pieces of debris that covered it, nothing would have indicated the spot where the ship lay that served as the tomb of four brave men.

Sir Owen lavished the most urgent care on the shipwreck victims. When the men had been dried off and fortified by cordials, the sole officer who had survived the catastrophe, the ensign, sounded the appeal.

Thanks to the restricted space of the *Sirius*, everyone had been able to save himself; only four names missed the roll call: Lieutenant Georges de Malher, the physician Lucien Sergeant, Midshipman Remi and the matelot Halgouët.

An hour later, the midshipman's body was recovered. As for the other three, it was known that they had been surprised in the holds; their bodies could not, therefore, be recovered until the day when the *Sirius* could be refloated…if that day ever came.

Sir Owen remained on the site of the disaster all day. He calculated the exact position of the place where the unfortunate ship had gone down. It was 36° 13″ north latitude and 24° 0 7″ east longitude, about a mile from the little volcanic islet of Syrtos. Having obtained that result, the commandant of the Investigator immediately set a course for Piraeus, in order to deliver the shipwreck victims to Admiral de la Rénolière, to give him the fateful news, and to surrender himself to the responsibilities that might weigh upon him.

When he had seen to everything, and watched the smooth, flat place disappear behind the *Investigator*'s wake, where he seemed distinctly to see a tomb—the place where a relative stolen from his affection and two brave strangers worthy of respect reposed in the eternal shroud of the mariner—he handed command over to Chanticleer, and went back to his cabin.

There his eyes fell upon the British flag draped over the head of his bunk. He tore it away and threw it on the floor, as if no longer to see the stain that a wretch had placed upon it. Then, sitting down at his work-table, he wrote an account of the terrible day in the ship's log.

And while he wrote the sober and faithful report, drafted in dry technical terminology, large tears fell from his eyes on to the thick vellum of the ledger.

V
Buried Alive

After Jean Halgouët had acquired the terrible certainty that she ship had sunk, he had a moment of dizziness, and took a few seconds to recover control of himself. We know that he was in a perilous situation: the iron chamber in which he was enclosed had, by virtue of the movement of the *Sirius*, tipped over on to one of her faces, so that the former floor was now a near-vertical wall. Naturally, that shift had provoked a displacement of all the objects stored in the compartment, notably the barrels, which had slipped to pile up against the fore wall, presently almost horizontal. As we have said, the Breton had instinctively clung on with his heels to the column forming a conduit of one of the pumps, and with his two vigorous arms he was supporting his two unconscious companions, clutching their clothing in his hands.

Although mentally stunned by the brutal revelation of imminent and inevitable death, he took account of what had happened, and was very clearly conscious of the movement of the *Sirius* as she sank into the water. The descent was exceedingly rapid, further accelerated by the invasion of the rear compartments, which, poorly closed or forgotten, had filled with water. The sensation of descent, of sinking, that he experienced only lasted a relatively short time, but its extent was naturally extended for the unfortunate man by the poignant anguish he was feeling. At every moment, in fact, he expected to see a panel give way and the water come to finish its work.

Suddenly, the hull of the *Sirius* experienced a relatively slight shock, and then Halgouët distinctly perceived a peculiar grating sound on the walls, a kind of soft rustling—after which the vessel stopped, motionless, still in the same vertical position. She had reached the bottom, and the matelot assumed that the prow must have lodged in a fissure in the submarine rocks.

The slightest surcease before the certainty of death is so welcome to the human soul that it immediately opens the door to the most implausible hopes. Halgouët, finding himself alive and seeing that the water was respecting the strange diving-bell in which he was enclosed, began to believe once again in the possibility of salvation, and rediscovered all his energy.

With infinite precaution, he let the two officers slide down on to the heap of barrels, then dropped on to it himself, after which he searched the doctor's pockets, hoping to find some cordial there. Although his lantern had gone out, his hand soon encountered a leather case, opened it, and recognized by groping a row of little bottles. He sniffed them one after another, and found that one of them contained ammonia. He immediately passed it under the doctor's nose.

Sergeant, who was only stunned, came round under the influence of the stinging sensation provoked in the nasal mucus by the bitter and volatile liquid,

"What happened?" he said. "And why are we in the dark?"

"In truth, Doctor, are you fully recovered, completely master of yourself?"

"Perfectly."

"Well then, this is it, in a few words. The *Sirius* has sunk, and we're imprisoned at the bottom of the sea, in one of her watertight compartments."

"Which is to say that we've escaped drowning temporarily, only to succumb to asphyxia."

"Probably."

"Surely, my friend, surely."

"Well, one never knows," said Halgouët, whose hope was tenacious.

"What about the Commandant?"

"He's beside us, unconscious, after falling off the ladder."

"So," said the doctor, "it's definitely written that I'll never see a cholera epidemic."

"Where are we?" said the voice of Georges de Malher at that moment, in the darkness.

"In a sticky situation, Commandant," Halgouët replied. And he repeated, briefly, what he had just told the doctor.

"So," replied the Commandant, "it's certain death in a matter of minutes?"

"At first sight, our compartment encloses about thirty cubic meters of air, which already wasn't very good. Perhaps we have enough for half an hour, assuming that we aren't inundated and drowned in the meantime."

"Well, my dear doctor," said Georges de Malher, "as all human aid is materially impossible, I don't see the necessity of enduring such a martyrdom, and if you have anything about you that will permit us to abridge it, I believe that we have nothing more to do than address a supreme thought to those who are dear to us, shake hands and then finish it off."

"Well, no," said the doctor, who had recovered his self-composure. "If God has preserved us thus far, why shouldn't he protect us a little longer? If he's saved us, it's because it doesn't enter into his divine plan to let us perish. It's improbable and absurd, I admit, but that's what I think."

"Me too," said Halgouët, who, in his robust Breton piety, easily admitted that Heaven might work a miracle in his favor.

"And then again, my dear friend, suicide isn't a solution. It's unworthy of a Christian or a soldier, and brave men like us ought not to think about it. Besides which, death by asphyxia isn't as painful as you might think. It's less painful than any poison I might have at my disposal. In those conditions, let's help ourselves. I think Heaven might perhaps help us…and if it decides otherwise, well, we'll have done our duty to the end. And just because one's at the bottom of the sea and no one is looking at you, that's no reason not to do one's duty."

These words were spoken in a grave tone, but without sadness; one recognizes by that a man who, being in the daily habit of battling with death, is unafraid and able to look it in the face. Such is the influence of the strength of the soul that the doctor's two companions felt their energy renewed, and they had a vague impression that the last word had not yet been said.

"And now to work," the physician went on. "Let's begin by making light. We'll sacrifice a little of our precious oxygen that way, but it's indispensable to see clearly."

Halgouët took some matches from his pocket, and struck one. They were able to find the lantern, intact thanks to the mesh protecting its spherical glass. They relit it, and set the wick as low as possible, just sufficient to shed a feeble light without consuming too much oxygen. All that took a certain time, and the atmosphere was beginning to become heavy.

As soon as the lantern was lit, the doctor picked it up and began searching.

"Let's see," he said. "We're in the third compartment from the prow, aren't we?"

"Yes, Doctor."

"Then we ought to find what we need to prolong our existence to a certain extent. I had two large crates stored here containing steel cylinders of oxygen under a pressure of eight atmospheres. You know that inhalations of oxygen are employed nowadays in medicine. It's a matter of finding those crates."

The search was difficult. All the merchandise embarked in the compartment had collapsed in a frightful pell-mell. There was no evident trace of any crates. It was necessary to move the barrels. Georges de Malher, still suffering the effects of the fatigue caused by his fall, could not muster his strength.

The air was becoming increasingly heavy, depressing all three men. Sweat was streaming on their temples, which were beginning to beat, while iron bands enclosed their heads and their respiration was becoming halting and oppressed. The little flame of the lantern was already burning low when the white wood of the two crates finally appeared under a pile of full sacks. They had no tools, but Quosé had his sturdy matelot's knife and, not without chipping it, contrived to open a breach in one of them.

As soon as the first cylinder was lifted out, the doctor opened the valve. A slight hiss was heard. In a matter of seconds the flame of the lantern became brighter, and their chests began to rise and fall more regularly; their malaise was considerably attenuated, but without ceasing entirely.

With his eyes fixed on the manometer fitted to the cylinder, the doctor followed the diminution of the interior pressure, in order only to release into the chamber the quantity of the precious gas necessary for the moment. As soon as the result was acquired, he closed the stopcock of the apparatus.

"That's better, isn't it?" he said. "Now we can begin unpacking the four cylinders we have at our disposal. I estimate that the contents of each one can renew our atmosphere for eight hours, so that's thirty-two hours we have before us. It's a matter of using them well. And when I say thirty-two hours, that's an overestimate it's necessary to include our lamp's share."

"Let's say that we have enough for thirty hours," said Halgouët, "and leave it at that."

"It's not much," said Georges.

"Certainly," said the doctor, while working with his companions to extract the cylinders, "it's very little for people who, sitting at a table in the Café Anglais, have begun to digest their oysters with the idea that they still have thirty years before them to stroll the boulevards, but it's enormous for poor devils like us, who, in good logic, ought by now to be sleeping their final slumber under a good many brasses of salt water."

"That's true," replied Georges.

"I'll even permit myself to say," Halgouët added, "that it's very encouraging. For in sum, five minutes ago we didn't even suspect that we had thirty hours in front of us."

"Right!" said the doctor. "There's our cylinders sorted out. We can pass on to another order of operations. You've doubtless noticed that, in spite of the oxygen, we're not yet breathing completely freely."

"That's the carbon dioxide," said Georges.

"Precisely. It's necessary to get rid of it."

"How?"

"We have here a number of barrels of lime, which I had embarked among the disinfectants. We're going to spread the lime out, which will absorb our carbon dioxide."

They had soon staved in a barrel, and spread the lime out everywhere they could, with the consequence that in a matter of moments, the atmosphere had become perfectly respirable again.

Georges de Malher immediately proposed that they organize "shipboard life," which provoked the first burst of laughter on the part of the three men that had animated their sinister prison. The doctor and the commandant both had their chronometers. Halgouët joined to that a respectable silver "onion" as large as a lady-apple "which he had from his grandfather and had never gone wrong." They carefully synchronized the three timepieces, in order not to lose the notion of time, and to regulate the emission of oxygen every half-hour.

Having taken that precaution, they began, at the commandant's suggestion, to make a minute examination of the walls of their prison. It was a matter of making sure that they were rigorously watertight, and seeing whether any defect might unexpectedly permit an abrupt invasion of water, obedient to the enormous pressure that their depth must being producing. That examination seemed all the more necessary since, now that calm had been restored, a slightly rustling seemed to indicate an infiltration.

They looked closely at all the joints, and recognized that the resistance to the water was as perfect as possible. Only three thin trickles were manifest in the starboard wall. They patched up two easily, with an improvised mastic made of flossed canvas, extinct lime and oil taken from the lantern. As for the third, the doctor let it run into a breached barrel "given that we can't do without water, even salt water, since one can make fresh water from salt water."

At that moment, Halgouët, alias Quosé, allowed a sonorous and prolonged yawn to escape, which he did his best to stifle "for the sake of discipline," but which he could not dissimulate.

"Pardon me," said the Breton. "Apologies, but it's the stomach. I'm beginning to feel hungry, and as the Commandant's *maître d'hôtel* must have gone the same way as the cook, my stomach's anxious. It'll gradually get used to waiting, I suppose. It's necessary not to hold it against me."

"It's certain," said Georges, "that it's a new dimension to the problem."

"We can probably resolve it," the doctor observed, "but I'd like to see you a little more cheerful, my dear Commandant."

"What do you expect, my dear Doctor? I can't help thinking, even in the midst of the present anguish, about my brave crew, who have doubtless perished. And I'm also thinking about my family!"

"For the sake of your family, my friend, the best means of thinking about them is to strive to preserve yourself for them."

"You're right."

"And as for the crew, they were in a better situation than us. Since, thus far, we've got out of it, there's no reason to mourn, until further notice, fellows who might perhaps at the present moment, be recovering their strength aboard the *Investigator*."

"In fact," said Halgouët, "why the devil are we at the bottom of the sea? What can have happened?"

"We'll figure that out later," the doctor put in. "For the moment, let's think about food. All the more so as, while thinking about that, we might perhaps find a means to prolong our existence, and—who can tell?— perhaps a means of saving ourselves."

"If Monsieur the Doctor continues to have ideas," said Halgouët, "I'll begin to recover hope for a good outcome."

"Well, I have a few ideas—except, alas, I don't have any tools."

"Tools?"

"Yes. But anyway, we'll see about that later. Say, Commandant, would you like to climb on to Halgouët's shoulders and get that little iron bar?"

Georges carried out that instruction.

"There! Good. Would you please, now, rap with the little iron bar on the wall above your head? That's the partition that separates us from the steward's stores. Our shipwreck, in turning the *Sirius* over, has elevated it to the dignity of the ceiling. Is the store-room inundated, yes or no? That's what we need to know."

After a certain number of raps struck on different parts of the surface, they concluded that the fourth compartment, containing the steward's stores—which is to say, the food supplies—had not been invaded by the water. It was a matter of making sure of that, by attempting a decisive experiment. For that it was necessary to pierce a hole—but as the doctor had said, they did not have any tools with which to proceed with that operation.

The three men racked their brains. None of them found a solution.

"In truth," said Quosé, having struck his hard Breton head with repeated blows of his fist, "I can't see any means on making a hole in it."

"Well, my friend," Sergeant replied, "Do you know any modern history?"

"Not much, Doctor—but there's nothing I don't know about the voyages of Ulysses, who, if my memory serves me right, sailed the regions in which we find ourselves in search of his island of Ithaca. If that can be of any use..."

"Not for the moment. Simply remember that Bonaparte, lacking everything, as separated from the plains of Lombardy by mountains far more terrible than that thin curtain of steel plate, and found a means of overcoming those frightful obstacles in order to go in search, on the other side of the Alps, of what he needed to feed and clothe his troops. Well, our task is much easier. We only have to pierce two centimeters of iron, and as we can only eat if we do, it'll be the very devil if we don't succeed in doing it."

"Just a moment!" exclaimed Georges. "I have a notion that during the loading, a crate of tools was sent down here."

"Are you sure?"

"Very nearly. I can see the crate: a big oblong box, in oak, on which the master carpenter, to whom it belonged, had the whim of painting two tricolor flags with crossed poles."

"Let's search, then."

Again they started shifting piles of sacks, barrels and crates, and after half an hour, they laid their hands on the precious parcel. With the aid of the iron bar they prized open the lid swiftly and unceremoniously—but then an immense disappointment succeeded hope. The box was not the carpenter's; it belonged to the master of arms. It contained breastplates, fencing-masks, an assortment of gauntlets, waxed thread for attaching buttons, iron wire for repairing masks, a dozen pairs of foils of different gauges, and two pairs of épées. Nevertheless, having emptied it out completely, they found a few tools necessary for the repair of broken foils: a hammer, a little vice, pieces of zinc for making welds, two or three files for smoothing metallic bandages, a few sticks of solder and a soldering lamp.

"All that's not much use for anything," said Georges de Malher, in a melancholy tone, when they had completed the inventory of the crate.

"You know, my friend, you're very prompt to get discouraged. On the contrary, we have here everything that we need for our experiment."

"In truth, Doctor, said Halgouët, "it's a pleasure to listen to you, but I confess, myself, that I agree with the Commandant."

"Well, my dear friends, we have steel foils here. We break one, we sharpen it with the files, we heat it up with the soldering lamp, and we temper it in the sea-water that we have at our disposal. That's the gimlet necessary to excavate the hole."

"That's true, but how do we activate such a gimlet in such a way as to give it the speeds of rotation and force of penetration necessary to penetrate two centimeters of steel?"

"We take another foil, which we bend into a bow, giving it for a string the iron wire that we possess. We loop the string thus made around the gimlet, and by moving the bow back and forth in the fashion of an Arab lathe, I'm strong enough to pierce a hole in the all of the food-store in less than twenty minutes."

The two pessimists were obliged to yield. The program was followed, step by step, and after barely half an hour the hole was pierced. Not a drop of water ran through the tiny opening.

"My dear friends," said Sergeant, "the store-room is intact." Philosophically, he added: "That is how brutal weapons can render services to science."

"*Cedant arma togae!*"[6] exclaimed Quosé, enthusiasm making him lyrical. "Except," he observed, returning to reality, "it isn't through that little hole that we can get hold of a single tin from the larder."

It was Georges de Malher who replied. Confronted by these results, and the incessantly-alert ingenuity of the doctor, he had come back to life. He had been gripped in his turn by the fire of the struggle, the delirium of that admirable combat with the impossible, so bravely accepted by the man of science who was facing the same frightful dangers. He exclaimed: "But the rest is mere child's play. We have an iron bar and a hammer. Since there's no water in the store-room, we'll find food there."

He chose one of the seams, filed a groove, engaged his lever therein, and struck it with a few blows of the hammer, redoubled over the head of the iron bar. Perched on the heaped-up barrels, Halgouët helped him, and took over the hammer when his arm became tired. Under those combined efforts, the iron plate gave way, and a few vigorous thrusts of the iron bar opened a gap sufficient for a person to squeeze through.

Then the two workers looked at the doctor, who, during their stubborn labor, had opened one of the oxy-

[6] Let arms give way to the toga (i.e., let military authority give way to civil authority). The quotation is from Cicero.

gen taps wide and was stirring the spread-out lime from side to side.

"What are you doing, my friend?" asked Georges.

"I'm helping you," the doctor said, "by giving you strength."

"But you're squandering our precious reserves of oxygen."

"Don't worry. Just go find us something to eat and drink. Then, his face suddenly brightening, pirouetting and clicking his fingers, he added: "If the sea will just leave us in peace! Oxygen! I have handfuls of it, if I can put it like that. Yes, I have oxygen! And something else with it! My friends, the little fellows are still alive!"

VI
Anything rather than slow death!

With his acrobatic agility, Quosé was the first to haul himself into the store-room. From there he held out his hand to Georges, who hoisted himself up after him. The doctor, mounted on the heap of barrels, passed them the lantern.

Naturally, the greatest disorder reigned within the narrow space. The storage-locker was, in fact, only one section of a compartment, the rest of which was occupied by the coal bunker, but, by reason of its very exiguity, the food supplies there were packed as if in a trunk. The tinned food, the boxes of biscuits, the casks of wine and the demijohns of alcohol had been crammed in by the steward in such a way as to utilize all of the space, so effectively that the disorder was more apparent than real.

The two explorers passed down to the doctor everything that came readily to hand: several boxes of biscuits, a large number of tins of corned beef, pork tongues, sardines in oil and dried vegetables, and then two demijohns of eau-de-vie, and, finally, in default of the casks of wine—which would not pass through the opening—fifty bottles of fine wine that were part of the officers' reserves.

"If we have to stay here," Quosé remarked, "At least we'll embellish our final days with the sampling of some famous vintages and a few bottles of champagne, which certainly had not been destined to be drunk on the sea-bed. That's a small satisfaction, you might say, but it doesn't lack originality. What's annoying is not to be sure of being able to tell the tale."

"By the way," called the doctor, from below, "Try to find me some oil."

"Oil? There! Boom!" shouted Quosé. "I've just found a nice barrel *Union des propriétaires de Menton*, it says on the label, *virgin oil*. Do you need anything else?"

"No—we have enough for some time."

"In that case, Commandant, if you'd like to go back down, you can help me get the barrel of oil down."

Georges let himself down into the lower compartment again. After having passed him the barrel, Halgouët got ready to do likewise when he felt a few drops of water fall on his head.

"Hey," he said, "it's raining. You wouldn't happen to have an umbrella?"

"What did you say?" asked Sergeant.

"I said that it's raining."

"Hold on, here's the hammer. Before rejoining us, try to sound your ceiling—which is to say, the partition of the engine-room."

"I'm on it."

Their ears cocked, the commandant and the doctor listened to the hammer-blows struck by Halgouët."

"It's full of water, isn't it?" said the former.

"Very full, Doctor."

"Then we can't take too many precautions. Send us everything that you have to hand."

Quosé did not have to be asked twice. There was a veritable avalanche of tins, boxes and bottles.

"Good," said the doctor. "Now come back down."

When the matelot had rejoined his two companions, the doctor said: "Now it's a matter of undoing what we've done."

The task was not easy, all the more so as the workers, fatigued by the emotions they had endured and the superhuman labor they had done in a thick atmosphere, were beginning to reach exhaustion. But Sergeant declared that it was urgent, and his two companions, submitting with a good grace to the ascendancy of his moral strength, set to work. They drank a glass of old cognac bought by the officers for on-board receptions, and then set about replacing the sheet metal that they had levered away.

While Georges and Halgouët employed themselves in that task, the doctor bent foils in a flame, shaped them into hooks, tempered them and passed them up to the others in order that they could pull the plate into place.

That labor lasted for about an hour. At the end of that time, there was only a slight gap between the metal sheet and its frame. Through the holes of the bolts that has been removed, the doctor contrived, with iron wire twisted into an eight-ply strand, what he called a suture-point; then, with the oil of which he now had an abundant supply, he made more mastic with the expended lime and threads of sackcloth. That stopped up the openings hermetically, and, beneath the surface that he had pierced, he spread a thick layer of cement, over which he applied two superimposed box-lids, supported by a column comprised by four barrels placed one on top of another.

When it was all finished, the doctor examined the ensemble with a satisfied expression.

"Now, my friends, we've certainly earned our dinner; we can sit down at table. What time do you have, Commandant?"

"Seven o'clock."

"Well, our meal is only an hour late; that's no reason to complain! Halgouët, you're promoted to the functions of steward. Give us, please, a tin of beef, some biscuits, and two bottles of champagne; we haven't stolen them."

"That's true," Halgouët replied, "but it's a bit close in the dining room. What if we were to open the windows a little?"

"You're right," said the doctor, and opened the tap of one of the oxygen reservoirs.

"Let's not squander it, Doctor!" cried Malher.

"How you do go on! Since I tell you that I have pockets full of oxygen...take that slice of beef that Halgouët has just carved so artistically, which he's holding out with the deference due to you. I'll uncork the champagne."

While speaking, the doctor cut the threads of wire that were retaining the silver cap of the bottle, and Quosé set out before the diners, on the barrel that served as a table, three tin-plate mugs that he had found in the storeroom. The cork sprang out, with its joyous celebratory pop, and at the same instant, as the cups were extended toward the French wine, a loud noise was heard: something akin to a formidable cascade falling on the ceiling of the narrow shelter where the three men were clinging on to life. It was the wall of the engine-room that had given way, allowing water to rush into the storage-locker

Georges and Quosé could not help putting their mugs down on the barrel again.

"Well, Quosé," said the doctor, "that was expected. I thought that the force of the steam produced at the moment of the invasion of the sea must have severely tested the engine-room bulkhead. That's why I wanted to seal the storage-locker. The water's over our heads, my friends, but it won't get through. Believe me, raise your glasses and let's drink to a health that the future will ratify." He gave his jovial voice a solemn tone and added: "Messieurs, I drink to the three missing men of the *Sirius!*"

And under the sound of the swirling water that was falling overhead, the three brave men calmly emptied their cups of champagne.

The meal, necessary as it was, was concluded in a hurry. Naturally, they said little, since they were eating rapidly. Nevertheless, for the first time, they exchanged a few ideas relative to the catastrophe, and the three prisoners found themselves in accord in attributing it to a collision. None of them, however, thought that the collision could have been with the *Investigator*, which had been following a course parallel to that of the *Sirius*. If Halgouët had known that Thomas Tingle had been at the helm at the moment of the disaster, he might have been able to explain the incident other than by an unfortunate accident, but he did not.

As for the closing of the hatch that had immured them, they were not astonished by that, and all three found the true reason for that terrible maneuver.

"Immediately after the collision, the first impulse of all the matelots within range," said Georges," must have been to close the watertight compartments in order to prevent the immersion of the ship. Our compartment was sealed by some crewman who was unaware of our present in the holds. In any case, all that is of merely platonic interest; it's not a matter of knowing how we got here, but how to get out."

"Good," said the doctor. "I like to hear you talk like that. We're going to set to work immediately, and even if the attempt we're going to make seems improbable, I'm not despairing of success. You feel fortified somewhat by the meal?"

"I'm ready to do anything you wish, my dear doctor," said Georges.

"And I'll work day and night to see the blessed dawn again, while I smoke my pipe on the mainmast of some vessel or other."

"Well, firstly, it's a matter of bringing a little order to this lumber-room in which we find ourselves, and of making an exact inventory of our resources."

They proceeded with that operation immediately, which took some time because of the entanglement of the packages, especially because of the defective lighting of the only lantern the workers had. Finally, at three o'clock in the morning, the barrels, classified according to the substances they contained, were tacked on top of one another in an orderly fashion. The boxes were stacked separately, and sufficient room remained in the chamber for the three men to move about freely.

As the clearance proceeded, the doctor made a note of the merchandise they rediscovered. When the organization was complete, he demanded imperiously that his companions sleep for two hours.

"Obey me, Commandant, and you too, Halgouët. Besides which, while you're asleep, I'll be able to work in tranquility." Light-heartedly, he added: "I don't like to have people around me when I'm, working."

They were obliged to obey. The doctor installed himself beside the lantern, his notebook in his hand, and started tracing calculations and chemical formulae on the pages—after which he headed for a large crate set aside on his instructions, which he set about opening.

It was one of the packages that he had loaded on to the *Sirius* with a view to installing his private laboratory. It will be remembered that that fraction of the cargo had been the object of special care on the doctor's part, and that he had carefully stowed the boxes in the corner adjacent to the wall of the store-room. Thus caught between three surfaces, they had simply slid at the moment of the disaster, and did not seem to have suffered much. Nevertheless, the doctor, hardened as he was, could not help his heart accelerating as he prized open the lid of the first box. It contained retorts, flasks and glass tubes, and if those precious instruments were broken, it was the end of all hope. It was for that reason, above all, that Sergeant had worked alone, in order to receive the first impact in case of misfortune.

When the lid was off, the doctor withdrew the thick layer of straw that covered the apparatus. The first object he felt beneath his hand was a fragment of broken glass, which inflicted a sight cut on his finger; that was a bad omen. In fact, he found himself in the presence of a heap of debris, and for a moment he thought that the entire contents of the crate had been broken by the impact. In spite of everything, however, he was not discouraged. He took out all the formless fragments, and with an inexpressible joy he found, carefully rolled up in sleeves of straw and oakum, which had preserved them, a number of matrasses, round-bottomed flasks and retorts in glass and earthenware, tubes, a few flasks, and several tubulatures. In a corner of the crate there were cork stoppers and a coil of rubber tubing.

His serenity restored, the doctor passed on to another phase of the search. It was a matter of finding out whether the distillation apparatus destined to procure pure water, either for purposes of medication or alimentation, were intact. About that, however, he was much less anxious. By reason of its primitive nature, that apparatus ought not to have suffered. He found it in good condition, and, as he did not need anything more, he did not occupy himself with anything further. As for the alcohol necessary for its functioning, he had three casks of it.

Once those results were acquired, he woke Georges de Malher.

"My dear friend," he said, "It's your turn on watch. You're going to stay awake for two hours while I sleep. Give us oxygen every two hours, stir the various beds of lime, and in order to utilize your leisure, arrange the various utensils I've exhumed in good order. When you're tired, wake Halgouët. As long as I can sleep for three hours that's all I need. "He laughed, and added: "When day dawns, we'll arrange our present existence definitively."

"Just one word, my friend," Georges relied. "Do you still have hope?"

"More than ever, my dear Commandant. We'll try everything to return to the human world."

"And to see those we love again! Oh, yes, Doctor, let's not seek merely to prolong a miserable agony. Anything, you see—anything—rather than slow death!"

VII
The Role of a Great Fortune in a Great Dolor

The day after the catastrophe, at eight o'clock in the morning, Admiral de la Rénolière was talking to the Commandant of the *Guichen* on the bridge when the officer, who had been looking through his binoculars momentarily at a vessel entering the harbor, handed the instrument to his superior and said:

"Look, Admiral; I'm not mistaken—that's the *Investigator* coming in."

Monsieur de la Rénolière took the binoculars and looked in his turn. "You're right," he said. "It's definitely the *Investigator*."

"But Sir Owen Townsend had announced his intention of going all the way to Beyrouth in company with the *Sirius*."

"Yes, it is odd. He must have changed his mind. Sir Owen might have thought that he was exposing himself and his crew to serious danger, followed by a great deal of inconvenience, and decided, with his English common sense, that British honor could do without the quixotic action that he was attempting. That wouldn't astonish me overmuch."

"Either that," replied the Commandant, "or he's suffered some damage."

"I don't think so," said the Admiral. "The yacht seems to be traveling at its normal speed." Having raised the binoculars to his eyes again, however, he went on: "But wait—look, my dear friend. Don't you observe something strange about the vessel? My eyesight is declining, and I might be mistaken. Take the binoculars."

"My God, yes," replied the officer. "I see that the *Investigator*'s sails are disordered, and the British flag on the horn and a French flag on the main-mast are both flying at half-mast."

"My dear friend," said the Admiral, "I regret what I just said; the *Investigator* is coming back because something bad has happened on board."

"Indeed—but I'm asking myself one question."

"Me too, and it's probably the same one: why is that French flag at half-mast?"

"Yes. Sir Owen isn't French, and if something unfortunate had happened on board, why associate our flag with it?"

The Admiral did not reply, but he went very pale, and the brief reasoning that the Commandant of the *Guichen* had just formulated immediately gave him the somber presentiment of a catastrophe whose nature and extent he did not dare to formulate.

"Commandant," he said, "you must be experiencing the same anguish as me. It's natural, isn't it, that I'm not going to hesitate at this moment over a matter of etiquette? Have the launch lowered immediately—I'm going aboard the *Investigator*."

In a matter of minutes, the order was carried out. Already, eight matelots were waiting, oars in hand, while the coxswain, standing up and armed with a crowbar, was ready to give it the initial impulsion. The Admiral, passing between two rows of officers respectfully baring their heads, had already reached the port when they saw a launch detach itself from the flank of the *Investigator*, traveling at top speed. Just as Monsieur de la

Rénolière was about to descend the ladder, the Commandant of the *Guichen* pointed that out to him.

"Sir Owen is in the boat," he said. "He's heading straight for the *Guichen*."

"That's right; I recognize Sir Owen. Haul the launch up again, and signal Sir Owen to come aboard."

The *Investigator* was no more than a hundred brasses from the *Guichen*, so the launch from the English yacht reached the stairway with a few strokes of the oars. Sir Owen climbed the steps stiffly, very pale but apparently very composed. When he arrived at the port he saluted the Admiral gravely. The latter returned his salute. Then, reading in his visitor's somber gaze the confirmation of the expected misfortune, he invited him to come to his private apartment.

As soon as they were alone, Monsieur de la Rénolière, still courteous in spite of his anxiety, advanced a seat for his visitor. The other refused it, and said: "Admiral, I have terrible news to announce."

"I expected as much, Monsieur, having seen the livery of mourning on your ship. Is it the *Sirius*?"

"The *Sirius* is lost."

"With all hands?"

"No. I saved almost all of the crew."

"Thank you, Monsieur," said Monsieur de la Rénolière, extending his hand to Sir Owen

The latter did not take it. "Don't thank me, Admiral," he said. "The rescue operation was only a minimal repair, alas. I'm the one who caused the loss of the *Sirius*."

"You!"

"Yes, me—or, at least, my ship. The *Investigator* rammed the *Sirius* in the fog and sank her."

"And it's to me, the man responsible for the ships that have been confided to me by France, that you dare to make that confession so calmly!"

"To you first, Admiral, by virtue of the painful virtue of courtesy; then to the maritime authorities, for I don't intend to deny any responsibility."

Master of himself as he was, the Admiral felt anger boiling within him.

"Oh, really, Monsieur," he exclaimed, "really!—it only required a bank of fog, which, according to what I've been told, only spent ten minutes on the surface of the sea, for the *Investigator* to ram and sink a French ship! You don't waste time, you Englishmen! In spite of the bell, the siren and the lights, you only required a momentary fog to destroy my poor *Sirius* and drown her crew!"

"I've told you that almost all of the crew was saved."

"Almost! Which is to say that there are men dead. And you want me to believe that this catastrophe was the work of chance, when you were sailing in convoy, and if you knew the ABC of the métier, the slightest diminution of speed would have been sufficient to prevent such a disaster! No, Monsieur, I don't want to attribute the loss of the *Sirius* to the presumptuous ignorance of a man who, because he's rich, thinks himself capable of commanding a ship. This collision is not an accident, Monsieur, it's a crime! The *Sirius* was probably in your way, you hit her, and that was all: you were the stronger, your ship the more powerful, and the *Sirius* presented herself side-on. And you simply won a small victory, devoid of glory, it's true, but also devoid of risk, which England will recompense, but the world will scorn..."

"Admiral!"

"Monsieur, I'm too much a mariner to be deceived. It's not to me that you'll dare to sustain that the ramming of the *Sirius* by the *Investigator*—in misty weather, it's true, but in s calm sea, and given that the two vessels were traveling on parallel courses—was a simple effect of fatality. Malevolence was the cause, and malevolence alone. Whether the crime was committed by you, I don't know, but you're the captain of the *Investigator*, and as such, responsible. If you didn't commit the crime, you weren't able to prevent it, and that's the same thing."

"Admiral," said Sir Owen, gravely, "I don't have the right to defend myself. Your patriotic anger is legitimate, and if it takes responsibility for the catastrophe that I would have given my life to prevent all the way back to my fatherland, I don't have the right to complain, pending more ample explanations. You're right, Admiral; the loss of the *Sirius* was not due to hazard; it was in fact the result of a crime, and I am indeed morally responsible. Four men have perished, and I shall never console myself for that."

"So you admit that a crime has been committed?"

"I admit it because it's the truth."

"Before anything else, who are the four men missing?"

"Dr. Sergeant, Midshipman Remi, Matelot Halgouët, and Lieutenant de Malher."

"Three valiant officers and one good matelot less! Four brave men stolen by you from France—which scarcely matters to you—and from their families, which ought perhaps to touch you more, for people must also love their families in England."

"Yes, Monsieur, and I feel it all the more because Georges de Malher was my relative, and I was extremely fond of him." As he spoke those words the Englishman's voice trembled, in spite of the superhuman effort he made to conserve the impassivity of his race and education.

In spite of himself, Monsieur de la Rénolière was moved. "Let's see, Monsieur," he said. "How did the catastrophe occur?"

"Oh, you can keep calling it a crime, Admiral. When we were enveloped by the mist I ordered the young sailor in charge of the helm to surrender it and replaced the novice with an experienced mariner named Thomas Tingle. The *Sirius* was then to our port. I therefore gave the order to steer to starboard. While I was ordering the engine to slow down, sounding the siren and ringing the bell, Tingle, against my clear and precise order, which he had understood perfectly, steered hard to port. I snatched the wheel from him, took his place and shouted to put the engine in reverse, but it was too late."

"And what have you done with Tingle."

"He's in irons, and will be disembarked in order to be put at the disposal of the maritime authorities. The investigation that I immediately carried out revealed that the sailor had in fact, been involved in an altercation with mariners from the *Sirius*, and that he had sworn to avenge himself. I've listened without complaint, Admiral, to the harsh things that you've said to me, because you were within your rights. I don't want to plead attenuating circumstances, but you might perhaps say to yourself that it isn't just to make England support the responsibility of the vengeance of a brute of a sailor. Certainly, it's shameful that such a man is English. It seems that, even for the coarsest natures, the community of dangers run on the seas ought to create a robust fraternity between all those whose lives are exposed to them, everywhere and under all flags. The crime of one wretch doesn't prevent English mariners from under-standing that fraternity. And I, Admiral...I...am ex-tremely unhappy."

Monsieur de la Rénolière, already shaken, was touched by the expression of profound dolor that Sir Owen had put into his words. In the cruel pain that was afflicting him, he found a sympathy for the grief of the man who, worthily and without prevarication, had of-fered himself to his legitimate anger. Again he extended his hand to the Englishman, and, when the other hesitat-ed, seized him.

"Well, Monsieur," he said, "if your matelot is a monster, that doesn't prevent you from being a worthy man. I've been hard, it's true, but think of what a chief might experience at the idea of losing thus, by an imbe-cile crime, four servants of his country!"

"I mourn them as you do, Admiral, if not more," Sir Owen replied, softly, "but I thank you profoundly for the evidence of esteem that you have just shown me."

The two mariners, who were very emotional, re-mained silent momentarily.

"Now," the Englishman went on, "I would like, to the extent that it is possible, to repair the damage that the *Investigator* has caused. I want to take personal respon-sibility for the reflotation of the *Sirius*. Furthermore, I want to render the last honors to the unfortunate vic-tims."

"Can they be recovered?"

"Yes, alas. I've determined the horrible circum-stances of their death. Without going into the details that the officer of the watch aboard the *Sirius* at the moment of the collision will give you—he was the last to leave the ship—this is how they died. Lieutenant de Malher, Dr. Sergeant and the matelot Halgouët were in the hold when the collision occurred. In the inevitable confusion that ensued, and without orders from the officers, someone closed the hatches of the watertight compartments. The unfortunate men were thus imprisoned, and must have perished when the water invaded the compartment. Their death must have been frightful, and I can't stop thinking about it..."

"Even more frightful than you suppose," the Admiral interjected. "The compartments of the *Sirius* are disposed in such a way as to resist the invasion of water from any direction. If the hatches were closed, they must, before the pressure of the water burst the walls, have found themselves in an enclosed space, and it's from asphyxia, for want of air, that they'll have perished."

"That's frightful!" said Sir Owen.

"Yes, because it was an inevitable, relatively slow death—death they saw coming without any possibility of rescue. And Midshipman Remi?"

"We recovered his body. He was submerged on the lower deck when, sent by the officer of the watch, he ran to warn the Commandant and his companions in the hold."

"Poor boy! Twenty years old and so much future! When one thinks that only a few hours earlier he was dancing so merrily aboard the *Guichen*."

"Spare me, Admiral, I beg you," said Sir Owen. "I'm at the end of my tether. I repeat that I would give my life if it would redeem the harm that has been done. I will give it, if necessary, with all I possess, to attenuate it. Help me now, and don't crush me anymore."

"You're right, Monsieur. Once again, pardon me. Let's see what you can do."

"Permit me to say what *we* can do, for I need your assistance."

"Count on me."

"First, we'll render the last duties to Midshipman Remi, whose body I've brought back to Piraeus. I've improvised a chapel of rest on my yacht; vigil is being kept over the brave French officer by officers of the *Investigator*, taking turns, and the poor boy will rest in holy ground. That, it seems to me, is the first duty to accomplish."

The Admiral nodded his head.

"Afterwards, I shall assemble here, at no matter what cost, the material necessary to proceed with the refloating of the *Sirius*. When I've brought the ship back to the surface, I'll tow her to Piraeus and we'll bury the mortal remains of the three brave men who died in the hold. After which, I shall make it a point of honor to return the ship to France in the same condition she was in when she left Piraeus."

Monsieur de la Rénolière seemed surprised by that declaration, made in the simplest fashion. "But Monsieur," he said, "it's me who has the duty of refloating the *Sirius*. It's with my government that I have to reach agreement on that subject, with the provision that the indemnities judged equitable will be reclaimed at a late date, through diplomatic channels."

"That's perfectly true in theory, but in this instance, with your permission, I'll pass over the formalities."

"But..."

"Pardon me. I want to acquit as soon as possible my double debt to humanity and your country. I intend, first, to recover your dead companions, then to restore your ship to you, without my country and I being obliged to submit to the shame of a reclamation, after that of having caused the catastrophe that we all deplore. Don't take away from me, Admiral, the sad privilege that I'm requesting. In any case, I'm free. Take your steps, and I'll take action."

"That's not regular."

"Perhaps not, but it's just. I'm only asking you for one great favor."

"Speak."

"My personnel will be insufficient. I don't know the Greek navy well enough to have full confidence in its collaboration, and in any case, I don't want to waste any time. Will you place at my disposal one of your engineers, and a few of your crewmen, including experienced divers? I only have two, and that's not sufficient."

"My God," said the Admiral. "People can say what they like, but I'll help you, Monsieur. How many men do you need?"

"Only the survivors of the *Sirius*."

"Naturally, they'll be under the orders of the engineer and the officers I'll give you. I can't place French subjects under the direction..."

"Of a foreigner. You're right. They'll only obey their officers, and I'll reach an understanding with them."

"Good, but one question. You're a mariner and a man of science. Do you sincerely believe that the *Sirius* can be refloated?"

"It will be difficult, but it's possible.

"You've marked the exact location of the shipwreck?"

"I've determined it. The ship went down at 24° 0 7″ east longitude and 36° 12′ 5″ north latitude. It ought to be at a depth of about thirty brasses."

"That's a lot."

75

"Undoubtedly, but we can try."

"Have you thought about the expenses it will be necessary to bear?"

"I've thought of it, and I shall bear them."

"Monsieur," said the Admiral, shaking Sir Owens hand again. "You're decidedly a worthy man." Then, with a sad smile that illuminated his somber visage briefly, he added: "I congratulate you, too, on being a rich man; for I've never appreciated the extent to which a great fortune like yours can attenuate a great dolor like ours."

VIII
For Salvation!

When he woke up, the doctor explained his plans to his companions.

"My dear friends," he said, "our task is divided into two very distinct parts: to survive here, and to get out.

"As regards the former, we're going to manufacture oxygen, and this is how:

"We have at our disposal various disinfectants. All of them contain oxygen. It's merely a matter of extracting it by the simplest methods. We've made our inventory; we possess calcium chloride, zinc sulfate, potassium chlorate, calcium hyposulfite, copper sulfate and potassium permanganate, in varying quantities. The necessity of loading the *Sirius* very rapidly obliged us to take everything we could find, and we can thank Heaven for that today. We should also have had a fairly large number of demijohns of sulfuric acid, but I've only found two bottles here; the others must have been stored in another part of the ship. Even so, what we have should suffice.

"I've calculated that we'll need nearly a week to make our preparations to escape. Now, a man consumes about 537 liters of oxygen every twenty-four hours. We therefore need, for the three of us, about 1600 liters of oxygen per twenty-four hours, which, for seven days, represents 11,200 liters. With the quantity of gas necessary for the combustion of the alcohol furnace and lighting, let's suppose that we need 16,000 liters. We'll operate on the potassium chlorate, which is a slightly dangerous manipulation, but simple. We'll be all right of we

77

take precautions. As a kilogram of potassium chlorate furnished 892 grams of oxygen, we'll only need, to give us the necessary quantity, 59 kilograms of chlorate. Now, we possess three barrels of fifty kilograms each. We therefore have ample to produce what we need to breathe for a week—and for three times as long, if necessary."

Halgouët opened his eyes wide, the long-haul captain who had educated him having entirely neglected to inculcate him with any notion of chemistry—which is excusable, having been much better informed himself with regard to the *Aeneid* than the reciprocal reactions of substances.

"Tell me, Doctor," he said, "Isn't potassium chlorate a kind of white powder."

"Exactly."

"And from that you can get respirable air?"

"Yes, or, at least, one of its essential components, oxygen, which enters into the composition of air to very nearly twenty per cent."

"And how will you get it out?"

"In a very simple fashion. I'll put the potassium chlorate in a retort, and heat it with the alcohol stove from the distillation apparatus that you can see over there in the corner."

"But if I'm not mistaken," said Georges, "That heating operation has to be carried out in special conditions. If not...."

"If not, it forms a crust on the surface of the molten mass, which leads to a perforation of the bottom of the retort. Then the potassium chlorate, falling into the fire, explodes and kills or wounds the operators. The Commandant is right to remind me of that. But to avoid such disagreeable accidents, it's sufficient to maintain the heat at a high temperature. It's precisely that circumstance to which I made allusion just now when I talked about taking precautions."

"And you think," Georges said, "that the alcohol stove will be sufficient to procure that high temperature?"

"I hope so, because I'll combine it with a particular mechanism—a sort of oxygen blow-pipe, that will stimulate the combustion, and for which, to begin with, we'll use part of the reserve that we have in our cylinders. Afterwards we'll aliment it by making use of the gap we obtain. So that's one point regulated.

"And to collect the manufactured oxygen?"

"That's quite simple. We'll adapt to the outlet of the apparatus I've just set up this rubber tube here. We'll invert one of the oxygen cylinders in the water, in which we'll pierce a minimal opening. Then we'll attach our rubber tube to the tap. As it's produced, the gas will displace the water in the cylinder, which will run out through the little hole. When the recipient in full we'll block that up with a stopper, close the tap, and we'll have a reservoir ready to renew our atmosphere. Thus, we'll have oxygen. But that's not all. As we breathe we exhale a certain quantity of carbon dioxide—about 21 liters an hour. Now, although the gas isn't toxic, it's inert, and asphyxiates in the same fashion as water, so it's important to absorb it. We've already started to do that; it's sufficient to continue by spreading lime, of which we have several barrels.

"Finally, we also exhale water vapor, but that won't inconvenience us. In fact, given the heat of the confined space in which we find ourselves, it will condense in droplets on the walls of the vessel that are in contact with the sea water, which is at a temperature much lower than our ambient environment, and we'll be able to sponge it away. Our house will obviously be a trifle humid, but that will be a mere inconvenience, quite tolerable."

"And in any case," observed Halgouët, who was always ready to make a joke, "we won't have the resource of complaining to the landlord."

"We are, in consequence, barring unexpected circumstances, virtually assured of being able to live here for several days. To tell the truth, I don't expect any complication to occur; the *Sirius* is an almost new vessel, the seams of her sheet metal are watertight. We have, it's true, since the storage-locker has been inundated, the mass of the water above our heads, but the upper partition is carefully sealed with a strong mastic that it's sufficient to maintain, and it's also solidly braced by the column of barrels we've set up. In all mines, pit-props that are far weaker support pressures that are much more considerable. Besides which, nothing prevents us from reinforcing our wedge."

"There remains the question of escape," aid Georges, who had approved the doctor's conclusions with a gesture."

"Exactly. In that regard, my dear Commandant, tell me whether you have some idea of how we might go about it."

"My God," the officer replied. "The problem is posed with such brutal clarity that there's not much to discus. There's only one means of getting out of her, and that's to pierce the side of the *Sirius* and to traverse the thirty or forty brasses of water that separate us from the surface. After which, assuming that we can get there, it still remains for us to find a boat close at hand to pick us up.

"With regard to the boat, I can't promise you that," Sergeant relied. "It's necessary not to demand too much. But strictly speaking, assuming, as you say, that we can reach the surface, we might not need a boat. In fact, at the moment of the catastrophe we had a small seemingly volcanic island to port, a short distance away, which you saw."

"I did see it, in fact. It's the islet of Syrtos."

"We could, therefore, reach it. And as they're very common in these parts, it certainly won't take more than a day for us to be collected from there by some vessel— a coaster or a fishing-boat. I don't see any great difficulty there, and if you'll permit me to say so, I think that in discussing that matter we're putting the cart before the horse."

"So be it—how do we get to the surface?"

"Let's hear what you think."

"We have three obstacles to overcome," said Georges de Malher, reflecting profoundly. "The first is the shock that will be produced when the water floods our redoubt through the hole we've pierced. In that regard, we seem to be in the presence of a dilemma that appears to me, at first glance, to be almost insoluble."

"What dilemma?"

"If we remove in one go, by some method yet to be found, a fragment of the hull large enough to give us immediate passage, the water, under that enormous pressure, will crush us. If we operate slowly, the water will enter gradually, but it will submerge us before we've finished contriving our exit."

"Very good," said Sergeant. "Let's suppose that first difficulty vanquished, and pass on to the other two obstacles."

"Let's assume, then," said Georges, "that we're out of the *Sirius*. We'll immediately have to support a formidable pressure. Let's assume, in fact, that we're at a depth of thirty brasses. The column of water rising above us would be nearly forty-nine meters high, which represents a pressure of about five kilograms per square centimeter. Our extended hand will support an effort of nine hundred kilograms in every direction. Will we be able to resist it?"

"Keep going."

"The final difficulty stems from the preceding one. Assuming that we can withstand that pressure, how will we retain the mental and physical strength necessary to swim up to the surface? How will we breathe during that ascension, short as it might be?"

"Is that all?" Sergeant asked, coolly.

"That's all, but it seems to me that it's enough."

"Well then, here are the solutions..."

Georges and Halgouët, who were anxious, as can be imagined, drew closer to the doctor. Georges was amazed by his composure. As for the Breton, he was no longer astonished by seeing the physician battle against nature, and he was listening with as much confidence as curiosity.

"You'll agree," Sergeant went on, "that if we can triumph over those three difficulties, we have serious chances of salvation. This is what we're going to do.

"I'll begin by declaring that your objections are perfectly just. We must, to begin with, avoid the terrible cascade that would be produced in our redoubt if we were to open a breach in it, and I shall set aside immediately, in the absence of better advice, the method that consists of allowing ourselves to be inundated slowly. This is how I think it's necessary to proceed: we'll draw on the sheet metal a square large enough to give us passage, and we'll file away the metal along each side of that square, in such a fashion as to be able to break away the square panel suddenly by means of a violent shock. When we're ready to emerge, we'll dispose a series of partitions all around the future opening and in front of it, made of all the wood we have—there's no lack of it. The water will break them one after another as it rushes in, and the shock we'll have to endure will be considerably deadened in consequence. It's certain that there'll be a unpleasant moment to get through, but that's a question of composure."

"And we're not here to amuse ourselves," said Halgouët.

"And how are we going to make the iron panel cut in the wall fall out?"

"With an explosive of my manufacture, for which I have the principal element in potassium chlorate."

"But we'll blow up too."

"No, firstly because we'll calculate the dose prudently, and secondly because the action of the explosive always operates in the direction of the strongest resistance; it's the iron wall to which we'll attach the cartridge that will absorb the shock and will be eviscerated."

"That's admissible," said Georges, after having thought about it briefly, "except that we'll probably be somewhat stunned."

"I don't believe so, but we'll arrange things so as to protect ourselves as best we can. It will be sufficient, in order for my plan to succeed, that we retain some shadow of presence of mind; the rest, in fact, will be almost automatic."

"Let's hear the rest."

"We possess large bottles of sulfuric acid. Several of the crates that are here are lined with zinc. We therefore have at our disposal what we need to manufacture hydrogen, decomposing water by the action of sulfuric acid on granules of zinc. Let's suppose that we can fabricate resistant balloons, inflate them with hydrogen and attach them to our shoulders. We can thus provoke a considerable rupture of equilibrium. In fact, you know that any body immersed suffers a loss of weight equal to the weight of the volume of water it displaces.

"If, for instance, we weigh 85 kilograms and our body displaces 60 liters of water, an excess remains of 15 kilograms, which is sufficient to make us sink if we don't swim. If, by means of a balloon filled with air—a bladder—I displace a further fifteen liters of air, my weight will be annihilated, so to speak. But if, with that same bladder, I displace twenty, I benefit in my turn from the excess—which is to say, from and ascensional force equivalent to the weight of five liters of water, which is five kilograms. It is, of course, necessary to deduct the weight of the balloon and the air itself. If I employ hydrogen, I obtain an even more evident effect, that gas being fourteen times lighter than air and slightly more than two thousand times lighter than water, and I no longer have to take account of its weight. Thus, with a balloon containing a hundred liters, I would obtain a considerable rupture of equilibrium, which ought, without our having to pay any attention to it—even if we were completely inert—to take us to the surface of the sea and cause us to arrive there in an interval of time, according to my calculations, of less than twenty seconds."

"All that's very accurate," Georges replied, "but how are we going to manufacture balloons sufficiently watertight and sufficiently resistant?"

"To tell the truth, we won't make balloons, but belts analogous to the rubber swimming-belts that are filled with air and of which people make use in learning to swim—except that ours will be much more considerable in their dimensions. To make them, we have at our disposal a bale of rubber-lined fabric, with which we provided ourselves, if you recall, in order to make draw-sheets for cholera-sufferers."

"But it's necessary to sew them."

"We'll make thread with oakum that was used to wrap the retorts and matrasses."

"I'll take charge of that," said Halgouët. "I know how to use a spindle, and although I've never spun at the feet of Omphale, I've seen my poor mother spin while my father was going for a spin of his own on the high seas in his fishing-boat."

"What about needles?"

"With metal wire and an oxygen blow-torch we can make some."

"And to render the stitches impermeable to water?"

"Ah! There I don't have a ready response," said the doctor, "but we'll see about making a varnish."

"Forgive me for insisting," said Georges, "but that's an essential point. If the stitches of our belts aren't rigorously resistant to the water, the pressure will flatten them instantaneously."

"Pardon me," said Halgouët, "but I've just had an idea."

"Let's hear it."

"It's more of a memory, but it might perhaps be useful. A few years ago, I was aboard the *Trident*, at anchor at Toulon after returning from a campaign. All my shoes were in a bad way, and I went ashore with the intention of getting them repaired more rapidly than could be done on board. A short distance from the Café du Commerce, I spotted a shop displaying a sign that said: *American Cobbler; repairs while you wait*. The owner put almost invisible patches on my soles, nor sewn but glued, and shoes repaired like that never let in water."

"Of course," said the doctor. "I know full well, my dear Halgouët, that there are impermeable varnishes—but I don't have to hand what I need to fabricate those of which I know the formula."

"That's just it—the cobbler in question made his magic glue with rubber—of that I'm sure. And he made his rubber dissolve in a liquid somewhat similar to oil, yellowish in color, which gave off an odor that would make an Eskimo village recoil—and God knows how difficult Eskimos are in matters of odor."

"A yellowish liquid, oily, with a very bad smell...but I know what that is!" exclaimed Sergeant. "I don't know why I didn't think of it. My dear Halgouët, you've saved us. The rubber I can obtain from my tubes and my fabrics, and as for the liquid, we'll manufacture it—it's carbon disulfide.[7]

"As for the pressure to which we'll be subjected, it won't surpass by much the extreme limits that a human being can tolerate, and besides, projected like bubbles toward the surface by the ascensional force of our reservoirs, we'll only remain in the deep layers for too brief a

---

[7] Pure carbon disulfide does not smell too terrible, but it is very difficult to manufacture without contamination by the foul-smelling carbonyl sulfide.

time for any serious disorder to be produced in our organism.

"Now, my dear friends, that we've resolved all the difficulties *theoretically*, I'll only add that, in order to prepare for any eventuality, we'll attach a respiratory apparatus to our belts, comprising an impermeable bag containing the quantity of fresh air necessary for a dozen inhalations and exhalations, in order to permit us to get our breath back after the invasion of the water. That apparatus will be fastened tightly to our mouths by a strip of rubberized cloth. It will have two tubes, one communicating with the air-bag, the other with the outside. Each one will be closed by a primitive valve made with a simple lead or tin pellet. We have tin in the master-of-arms' box.

When we breathe in, the air-bubble in the tube will collide with and lift up a little abutment, giving passage to the summoned air through the hole in a diaphragm on which it normal rests. The one in the free tube will be applied oven more forcefully to the diaphragm set above it. When we breathe out, the reverse phenomenon will occur; the bubble in the atmospheric conduit will press against the orifice and close it. The bubble in the free tube will cede by a few millimeters until a tiny abutment will allow passage to the expelled air, and under the double influence of the pressure of the water and the following inspiration, will come back to close the rubber diaphragm hermetically."

The doctor suddenly changed his tone and held out his hands toward his companions. "Are you convinced, my dear Georges, and you, my brave Halgouët?"

"Me?" cried Halgouët. "I'm listening to you like a god." A little more, and he would have kissed the extended hand.

"And me," said Georges de Malher, responding to the grip. "I admire you, and I'm yours, because for me, you personify mental energy, and it would be unjust if so much simple courage, composure and determination were expended in pure loss. My dear Sergeant, I have every confidence in you."

"In that case, my friends," said the doctor, taking off his jacket and rolling up his sleeves, "to the laboratory! Let's work hard, and open our penultimate cylinder of oxygen. It's time!"

IX
The Preparations for Reflotation

Sir Owen, standing modestly to one side, had followed the funeral procession of Midshipman Remi, who
had been escorted, in addition to the civilian and military
authorities of Piraeus and Athens, by delegations from
the ships of all nationalities that were in the harbor. All
the mariners from the *Investigator*, in their white cotton
uniforms, with crepe armbands, had taken their places in
the procession, but Sir Owen had left the leadership of
the contingent to his officers and had mingled with the
crowd. At the cemetery, after the speeches, when everyone else had gone, he deposited a silver palm on the officer's grave. Then, prey to sad thoughts, he headed for
the exit.

As he was about to go through the gate, a French
matelot who was standing nearby advanced toward him.

"Excuse me, Commandant," he said, "but it is the
captain of the *Investigator* to whom I have the honor of
speaking?"

"Yes, my friend. Do you have something to say to
me?"

"I would like to say something to you, but I can see
the Admiral approaching, and I'll retreat. Only, as an
effect of your generosity, Commandant, it would be very
good of you to give me a signal when you've finished
with the Admiral."

And the matelot moved away, without even waiting
for an answer. In fact, Monsieur de la Rénolière had also
been waiting by the gate of the cemetery, and, surround-

ed by twenty officers in full dress uniform, he was heading toward Sir Owen.

"Monsieur," he said to him, "I didn't want to let that sad ceremony finish without giving you a testimony of esteem." He turned toward the general staff. "I know—we all know—that you are enduring the pain of a fatality that you have not merited. I will reproach myself for not having brought some consolation for the pain that you are so visibly experiencing, and I can tell you that all my officers join with me in expressing their heartfelt sympathy."

In spite of his self-possession, Sir Owen was profoundly moved. He took the Admiral's extended hands, shook them, and only found in his heart the very simple response: "You are true Frenchmen, Messieurs."

And while the cohort withdrew, after a respectful salute, the Englishman remained in place, his eyes staring, gratefully, at a tricolor flag veiled with mourning that was floating in the window of a French house.

At that moment, the matelot came toward him again and said: "Excuse me, Commandant, but now that the Admiral has gone, may I speak with you?"

Sir Owen looked at the stubborn interlocutor attentively. He was a short, thin man, but wiry, with a bronzed complexion and strange blue eyes beneath black hair.

"What do you want, sir?"

"This. It appears that you have the intention of refloating the *Sirius*. You've asked the Admiral for divers. You've been given two, Martial and Fricourt. They've brave lads, very solid, but you see, all boasting apart, they're not as useful as me."

"Ah! You're a diver?"

"A little; I've even worked in the port of Lorient under six brasses of water for hours on end, and the pump, hard-working as it was, became fatigued more rapidly than me."

"And you want to work on the reflotation of the *Sirius*?"

"Well, as an effect of your generosity, it would give me great pleasure if you were to ask the Admiral for me."

"I'd like to, since it's your métier, and I don't think the Admiral will refuse. I'll give you the high pay that I'm offering the other divers plus bonuses. I'll talk to Monsieur de la Rénolière tomorrow morning. Come and see me aboard the Investigator in the afternoon."

"Thank you, Commandant. The high pay, you know, is only of partial interest to me."

"Really?"

"Yes. Oh, I won't refuse it—but the thing is, I've been a friend since childhood of Jean Halgouët, alias Quosé, and his parents were very good to me, at one time. It's necessary to tell you that Jean's late father had a brother, who was a mayor's deputy in Muzillac, in Morbihan, in Brittany. And thanks to Papa Halgouët, who mentioned me to his brother, I got a bursary to Vannes, which served for my education, until the fourth year."

"Perhaps that's a lot for a coastal fisherman," said Sir Owen, who could not help smiling.

"Yes, but it was because I haven't only been a fisherman, Commandant, I spent who years as a so-called apprentice pharmacist. I was, to be honest, just a laboratory assistant to the pharmacist in Muzillac, but as he didn't have a pupil and often went hunting, I stood in for him."

"Very good—but I don't see what that education has to do with your being a meritorious diver."

"It's because I liked the sea a lot—the strange Breton Ocean that never wears the dame face two days running. Whatever the weather, between two eye-lotions or two pill-boxes, I'd go to take my bath in the big waves and stay for an hour in the water, practicing diving for as long as possible, to a whim. I collected a lot of slaps from the tails of porpoises, but it never corrected me, so one day, I left my boss there and joined the navy. As I had pleasure, true pleasure, in seeing the sea from underneath, as it were, I trained as a diver, and with my habit of holding my breath for as long as I wished, it was only child's play for me. With the result, at the end of the day, that I'd be very glad to contribute to finding my poor old Jean Halgouët, even dead, since there's no means of finding him otherwise. All the English aren't evil devils, are they, Commandant? And you have the air of being a worthy man, even though you sank our lovely *Sirius*. It was probably that you weren't able to do otherwise. One does what one can, we aren't princes..."

And on that philosophical conclusion, the matelot stopped, his feet squared, rolling his beret between his fingers.

Sir Owen, interested and touched, let the final compliment pass without flinching. "What's your name, my friend?" he asked.

"Yves Poulpiquet, Commandant."

"And you're embarked...?"

"Aboard the *Surcouf*."

"Good; if it only depends on me, you'll come to help us. Tomorrow, then, aboard the *Investigator*."

"Thank you, Commandant. I'll be there."

With that, the matelot saluted, turned on his heel and drew away. For his part, Sir Owen returned to the town, to which he was summoned by other concerns.

He immediately set out on campaign to assemble the equipment necessary for the reflotation of the *Sirius*. Thanks to the Admiral's support and the generosity with which the tore the pages of his check-book, he succeeded quite rapidly in getting together the materials he needed. Nevertheless, it took him a full week to complete the task.

Every time he found one of the machines he required, in the workshop of a shipbuilder or a manufacturer, he simply bought it, without haggling over the price that was asked of him. If the device was in poor condition her hired workmen, on no matter what conditions, who worked day and night to repair it. He thus procured, either with the collaboration of the Greek government or by addressing himself to private industry, fifty metallic pontoons of various shapes and sizes, and collected a vast stock of buoys and moorings, extraction pumps, kilometers of solid chains, and improved diving-suits with all their accessories. In eight days and eight nights, the Commandant of the Investigator scarcely got a few hours sleep.

The French officer of the maritime engineers who was assisting him was literally exhausted, but Sir Owen seemed to be made of steel. He had requisitioned, at triple pay, all the available workmen in Piraeus and Athens. All the pontoons had been carefully visited, tested and examined in every joint. While the metalworkers bolted the doubtful seams and reinforced walls that were too weak, and caulkers sealed them in order to ensure that they were rigorously watertight, fitters bored threaded holes in them destined to receive the screws of the pump-conduits, and powerful hooks to which the chain would be attached. The same was done for the buoys with which Sir Owen hoped to refloat the *Sirius*.

Reflotation operations are extremely delicate, and there is no general technique, so to speak. The means employed vary according to circumstance. When a ship has run aground almost at surface level, as recently happened at Le Havre with the *Touraine*, which sank at the harbor entrance after a wave drove her against the jetty, one can utilize cranes either mounted on powerful pontoons or fix points on the shore aiding their effect by lightening devices disposed around the vessel. Those lighteners are hollow bodies full of air, which are attached with chains or cables to the hull of the vessel, the combined effect of which sufficiently relieves the mass of the submerged ship by provoking a rupture of equilibrium.

When the vessel has sunk to a shallow depth, and is easily accessible by means of diving-suits, one can, if she is intact, seal her completely, rendering her as watertight as possible, after which the water she contains can be removed by means of pumps, replacing the water with air. It is easy to understand that a vessel thus emptied will return to the surface of her own accord.

Finally, when the ship to be refloated in resting on a relatively profound bed, and the means described above cannot be employed, one has recourse to watertight pontoons. If possible, divers pass chains under the hull of the vessel. Then pontoons full of water are sunk, which are attached to those chains. Subsequently, the water is pumped out of the pontoons, which become, so to speak, as many bladders around the mass of the sunken ship.

It is not always possible to pass the chains under the vessel; in that case they are attached as solidly as possible to the resistant parts of the carcass—and it is in that case that the divers must deploy all their courage and all their professional skill. The problem is already difficult enough when those brave workmen are operating at a normal depth; it becomes even more arduous when, under the pressure of deep layers of water, exposed to congestion, their ears buzzing and their chests tight, it is necessary for them to retain sufficient composure to orientate themselves in the midst of debris, moving in a resistant environment, being careful not to allow their air-supply tubes become entangled in the rigging and the broken equipment, and choosing the places favorable to the attachment of their chain, with points of support sufficiently robust to resist the effort and not break at the moment of the decisive pressure.

The question of divers was the one that, quite rightly, worried Sir Owen and the engineer most. The Commandant of the Investigator had seven experienced men at his disposal: a Greek mariner, two civilian workmen from Piraeus, one matelot from the yacht and three Frenchmen, including Yves Poulpiquet, whom the Admiral, at his request, had placed under his orders. Although they were accustomed to working under water, however, he could not think without alarm about the formidable pressure of five atmospheres that those essential auxiliaries would have to withstand. He judged it appropriate, therefore, to obtain diving-suits of a special type, which could, he believed, neutralize to some extent the effect of the layers of water, and permit underwater explorers to be supplied with compressed air.

It is well-known that a ordinary diving-suit is composed of an impermeable garment, closed at the wrists and ankles in such a way as to prevent any introduction of water, Around the neck, the garment is fitted with a steel collar with a screw-thread. On to that thread is screwed a metal helmet, enveloping the head, pierced with openings fitted with thick glass windows, themselves protected by grilles. A rubber tube brings respirable air into the helmet, driven by a pump, and an exit-valve permits the release of vitiated air. A communication cord connected to be diver's chest permits him to send the necessary signals, either to speed up or slow down the pump or to bring him back to the surface. Finally, a mass of lead suspended around the neck like an enormous medallion, and lead-soled boots facilitate immersion in spite of the resistance of the water.

It is easy to understand that, in those conditions, the pressure of the air sent into the envelope surrounding the diver must be equivalent to that of the water acting upon it. Under thirty brasses of water the diver has to breathe at a pressure five times greater than normal. He would not be able to do so if the apparatus were constructed in such a fashion as not to exercise any resistance to external pressure other than that of the air that it is storing.

It was by virtue of that reasoning that Sir Owen had been led to have diving suits of a particular kind constructed. Their fabric was composed of three layers of impermeable fabric, welded together by rubber varnish. All the seams were rendered impermeable by means of the same varnish. Thus far, apart from the unusual thickness of that triple fabric, there was nothing very new in the apparatus, but what differentiated it from all those that had gone before was the internal framework that the knowledgeable Englishmen had had fitted. The fabric was, in fact, supported by a veritable skeleton, made of supple and resistant steel springs, which followed the rounded contours of the body and limbs. The man was his protected by a kind of armor capable of resistance in its own right, without being supported by the pressure of the internal mattress of air, to the force developed by the layers of water.

At first, the engineer had raised a few objections, the principal one being that it had never been done, and that if the procedure were any good, the manufacturers of diving-suits would have been using it for a long time. Sir Owen, however, with figures in hand and supported by all the text-books of applied mechanics in the *Investigator*'s library, demonstrated to his auxiliary that solid fabrics supported by metallic carcasses could resist much more considerable pressures, and the engineer gave in.

In brief, after eight days of superhuman labor, the reflotation convoy was ready to depart. The weather was serene, the sea calm. At midnight, everything was finished. At daybreak, they were to set sail.

Then, for the first time, Sir Owen, exhausted, went down to his cabin to sleep.

He had scarcely gone in when a launch drew alongside the *Investigator*. A man came up on to the bridge and asked to deliver an urgent letter to the Commandant. That letter, which a delicate courtesy had led the postmaster of Piraeus to send to Sir Owen in spite of the late hour, was conceived as follows:

My dear Uncle,

In the immense grief that I feel, whatever the causes of the catastrophe that has occurred might be, I have only one thought—the same one that you have testified to me in your letter: to recover the body of my unfortunate husband. I am leaving tomorrow to join you.

Your affectionate niece,

Harriet de Malher.

Sir Owen immediately summoned one of his officers. "Lieutenant," he said to him, "Here's a check for five hundred pounds. Go ashore, find a steamer, charter it, and instruct its master to place himself under the others of Madame Harriet de Malher. As soon as my niece is aboard, let the steamer come to join us near the islet of Syrtos, whose position you know. Finally, as Madame de Malher is *en route* and I don't know, in consequence, where to send a dispatch, have a letter addressed to her deposited at all the major hotels in Athens and Piraeus, giving the name of the vessel that is waiting for her. We depart at six o'clock in the morning, Lieutenant, so you have five hours ahead of you."

"That's fine, Commandant. It will be done."

At half past five the lieutenant came back aboard the *Investigator*, and met Sir Owen as the latter was coming out of his apartment.

"Well, Monsieur?"

"Wall, it's done. The steamer I've chartered in ready, and Madame de Malher can embark as soon as she arrives on the *Miltiade*."

X
The Prison without Prisoners

At sunrise, the convoy destined to refloat the *Sirius* put to sea.

Its appearance was utterly strange, and in spite of the early hour, half the population of Piraeus, accumulated on the quays and jetties, was watching the departure of that singular squadron.

The pontoons had been divided into two groups of twenty-four, arranged in pairs thank to solid cables. Each of the groups was towed by a steamship. The *Investigator*, at the head, was leading the convoy. To her flanks was attached a bizarre assemblage of buoys of all shapes and sizes. It had been necessary to take minute precautions to avoid the pontoons colliding with one another under the influence of the waves, which would soon have damaged them and put them out of action. The mooring cables that linked the couples together were sufficiently long. Furthermore defenses in the form of cushions of rope garnished the walls of the floating caissons, in such a way as to avoid collisions. Finally, aboard the *Investigator* and the two steamships, a crew, relieved every three hours, was continually on watch, equipped with grapnels and crowbars, ready to put a launch to sea at the first sight of trouble and take their place there.

The crossing was effected without difficulty, somewhat slowed down by the convoy in tow. It took thirty-six hours to reach the area where the *Sirius* had sunk. It was then a matter of determining the exact spot where the wreck lay. The field of exploration was relatively narrow, by reason of the bearing carefully taken by Sir Owen before leaving the scene of the disaster. Given the depth however, a certain further loss of time would have been expected if the Englishman—who kept up to date with all scientific discoveries in spite of his time spent at sea—had not had the idea of utilizing an apparatus recently invented by an English officer, specifically designed for searching for submarine wrecks. The French engineer had not yet heard mention of that ingenious application of electricity. Sir Owen explained the principle and its functioning to him.

"Do you know the game of tongs, which has provided amusement in drawing rooms since time immemorial?"

"Yes. I played it when I first joined the navy, in the home of the Maritime Prefect of Lorient. It's a matter of finding an object hidden in the room. One person holds a pair of tongs and strikes them with a key. When the seeker gets close to the hiding-place one strikes there tongs harder, when he draws away one reduces the sound produced."

"Exactly. Well, we're going to find the *Sirius* the same way."

"That's very simple—but what will replace the tongs?"

"A telephone."

"And who will speak into the telephone?"

"The *Sirius* herself. We let a metallic wire down into the water, with a telephone receiver at the end on board, and a coil at the end under the water. The latter is placed between two coils through which equal induction currents are flowing. They cancel one another out and the instrument remains silent. But if a mass of iron is in proximity of one of the lateral coils, the current in that one is reinforced, the equilibrium is broken, and a current id developed in the median spiral; in consequence, the telephone emits a sound, which increases in intensity as it gets closer to the metallic mass—which is to say, the submerged vessel, and—becomes weaker as it draws away You can see that it really is the game of tongs. I have an apparatus with me, which I had put together in Athens, and we're going to use it immediately."

Indeed, having allowed the coils linked to the telephone down into the water, the Investigator began to describe a series of circles over the area to be explored, and it did not take long to discover the location of the *Sirius*. A number of soundings confirmed the discovery, and the tallow on the weight brought back imprints and tiny items of debris that left no doubt.

The following morning, the divers commenced their perilous and difficult task. In spite of the improvements made to the diving-suits by Sir Owen, four of the men were unable to reach a depth of twenty brasses. Of the other three, two—the Greek mariner and an Englishman—succeeded in reaching the wreck, but were obliged to return to the surface immediately. Only Poulpiquet was able to remain under water for a further quarter of an hour, and Sir Owen then blessed the lucky star that had put him in his path. Without him, the operation would have been interrupted, and it would have required several days to find divers endowed with a greater force of resistance—which would certainly have been difficult.

When the brave man came back aboard, blood was leaking from his nose and ears.

"It's because it's a long time since I've gone down to such depths, you see," he told Sir Owen, "but I'll soon adapt. A quarter of an hour under that pressure, to begin with, is already good. Except that I can't do everything on my own; the comrades need to train. If five of those who've gone down can get used to keeping me company for a few minutes, I think we'll succeed, but it will inevitably take longer if there aren't as many of us.

"In the meantime this is what I was able to see. The *Sirius* is almost vertical, nose down, with her prow embedded in the sea-bed, which seemed to me to be made of clay. On the starboard side the ship is buried all the way to the rip that the Investigator made. To port her flank is masked to a considerable height by a protrusion of the bed, which rises steeply at that point and continues sloping upwards in the direction of the islet of Syrtos, of which it's probably an extension. That's all I saw for today."

"That's a great deal, my friend," replied Sir Owen. "I'll remember you, be sure of that. We'll set to work immediately."

The two steamships dropped anchor above the *Sirius*, and then began the immersion of the pontoons, filed with water in advance. The operation was carried out by means of derricks emerging from rudimentary cranes established aboard the two vessels, which permitted the caissons to be lowered gently to the required location. They began with the ones that, being placed at the *Sirius'* prow, could rest directly on the bed, the descent of which did not require, in consequence, the collaboration of the divers. In the meantime, the latter trained.

By the morning of the third day, Poulpiquet was able to remain at the depth of the *Sirius* for half an hour. The two men who had reached the wreck on the first attempt could resist a sojourn of eight or ten minutes. As for the other four, they had been obliged to give up; one of them, after a further trial, remained seriously ill.

The position of the wreck did not permit chains to be passed under her keel; they would have slid off under the effort of traction as soon as pressure was imparted by the empty pontoons. That possibility had been anticipated, however, and the divers had enormous hooks and robust grapnels are their disposal, which they fixed everywhere that the resistance of the hull seemed to be capable of standing up to the effort. Then they linked those crampons by means of powerful chains to the pontoons, which were fitted with hooks of their own to receive them. Gradually, the *Sirius* was garnished with a crown of caissons and buoys. Those which were to be attached to the more elevated parts were immersed to the required depth by the derricks. On a signal from the divers, the descent stopped at the point they thought appropriate, and, resuming ten times over if necessary, they were attached to the flanks of the *Sirius*.

After a mere week's work, thanks to the precautions taken by Sir Owen and the improvements that he had made in the equipment, that first phase of the endeavor came to a conclusion.

It now remained to remove the water from the pontoons and replace it with air. That part of the work gave Sir Owen serious anxieties. The scientist had naturally understood from the very beginning that he could not make use of ordinary pumps to empty the caissons, which were supporting a pressure of five atmospheres. It would have been necessary to employ pressurized pumps or turbines, the deployment of which, given the circumstances, was impossible. Thus, Sir Owen had decided, in collaboration with the engineer, on a bold method that might succeed, and ought to, in theory, but whose results were as problematic as those of any untried experiment.

The *Investigator*'s boilers, established under the scrupulous supervision of her owner, were exceptionally powerful, even though the yacht was, as we have said, a hybrid vessel designed to navigate by sail or steam at will. We have already had one example of that resistance when Sir Owen had blocked the valves in order to keep up with the *Sirius* at the beginning if the voyage. It was a matter of taking advantage of that circumstance, to pump high-pressure steam into the submerged pontoons, and to make use of that to drive back the column of water in the exit tube. The resistance to be vanquished being five atmospheres, it was a matter of introducing steam into the caissons at a superior pressure in order to expel their contents.

It remained to be seen whether the caissons could support that pressure themselves, but Sir Owen had had them reinforced internally by stays and externally by strong hoops; in addition, their number was greater that was strictly necessary to displace the required volume of water. The success of the operation would not be compromised by the rupture of a few of the pontoons. The greatest difficulty was delivering the steam though a tube that was both sufficiently flexible and sufficiently resistant.

The scientist had resolved that difficulty as best he could, given the limited time that he had had to make his preparations. The connecting tubes—of which there were three—were composed of six sections varying between two and twelve meters in length, which was sufficient to permit them the necessary undulations. The joints were formed by very thick leather casings, lined internally with bracelets of imbricated copper and externally by an extremely resistant fabric formed by several layers of interwoven steel wire. At each extremity, a threaded coupling permitted adaptation to the pontoon and the outlet of the steam-engine, and leather collars made sure that the joints thus formed were watertight. Finally, the entire tube was lined with a fabric of tight cord, over which was an insulating coating designed to avoid the loss of steam, thus maintaining the pressure.

It was with real anxiety that the system devised by Sir Owen was tried out. The entire crews of the three vessels, gathered on the decks, the spars and the rigging, followed the operation. Not a word was heard other than the commands. By means of derricks installed aboard the Investigator, the tube was slowly lowered; then, when it was entirely unrolled, a second was send down, destined for the expulsion of the water and its subsequent replacement by air. As soon as the two tubes had been unrolled, three divers plunged into the water. In sixteen minutes they had fitted the screw-threads to the caps of one of the pontoons, and then came back up. The steam tube was connected to the boiler; the other remained suspended from the side of the ship.

"What's the pressure?" Sir Owen asked, speaking into the engine-room microphone.

"Eight atmospheres, Captain," replied the engineer.

"That's good; is the tube securely fitted to the outlet?"

"Yes, Commandant,"

"Open the valve!"

Sir Owen was gripping the engineer's arm, anxiously. They were both pale. Science is so impassioning that those two men, at that moment, were experiencing the same anguish as if it were a matter of bringing back the three missing men of the *Sirius* alive.

A minute went by; no water emerged from the second tube. Sir Owen began to despair.

"Courage!" the engineer said to him. "The steam cooled on contact with the water and condensed on arrival. It needs time to heat up the surface."

Another minute went by. This time Sir Owen had come to believe that the game was definitely lost, when a sound of seething was suddenly heard, and a column of water ten meters high rose majestically from the tube.

In spite of his British stiffness, Sir Owen threw himself into the engineer's arms. "Finally!" he cried. "If I can't return your three brave men, I'll give them a tomb, and at least I'll give you back the *Sirius*."

From that moment on the reflotation followed its regular course, without any serious accident. Only three caissons burst under the pressure, and a few were distorted without breaking. All the others resisted, and as they filled up with air the position of the *Sirius* changed. First of all, she was disengaged from the hole in the clay in which she was embedded, which matched her contours rigorously. The consequence of that movement was that she resumed a near-horizontal position. At the same time, she rose up through the water to a depth of less than twenty brasses, which permitted the divers—with the exception of the sick man—to be joined by three other novice workers. Poulpiquet spent half his life under water, directing his companions with the aid of a system of signals that he had taught them. Thus, the work progressed rapidly.

As soon as the vessel had quit her primitive position, Poulpiquet made a tour of her. That day he came up precipitately and when his helmet had been unscrewed

Sir Owen saw an expression of astonishment painted on his face.

"What's the matter?" he said. "Have you made a discovery?"

"Yes, Commandant—a very bizarre discovery."

"What?"

"It was to starboard that the *Sirius* was rammed, wasn't it?"

"Yes, of course."

"Well, there's another rip in the hull to port, considerably behind the first. It's at the level of the third watertight compartment—the very one that Monsieur de Malher and his companions were in at the moment of the disaster."

"Is it large?"

"Very large. About half a meter in diameter."

"The ship might have struck a spur of rock as she went down."

"Perhaps..."

"You don't seem to like that explanation?"

"It's just that it doesn't satisfy me, Commandant. The opening has a distinct shape: it's square. One might almost think that the ship had been scuttled."

"Come on—that's not possible. It's probably a plate of sheet metal that has come away in its entirety."

"Yes; that's possible...in fact, on reflection, you must be right. In any case, the unfortunate prisoners won't have died of slow asphyxiation by bad air. They'll have drowned in the hold..."

"Oh, my friend," said Sir Owen. "It's almost a relief to think that they perished in that way. You didn't try to go in through the opening?"

"Yes, but I didn't succeed. It's obstructed by a tangle of material of various sorts. It would have required long, hard labor. By tomorrow, I think the vessel will be almost afloat. It'll be easier then to get into the hold through the hatch."

"That's true. We'll get there as quickly, with less difficulty."

The next day, in fact, under the ascensional force of all the air-filed pontoons, the masts of the unfortunate ship emerged. Shortly thereafter, the bridge and the funnels appeared in their turn, but the *Sirius* stopped a meter below the surface of the water, as if the sea did not want to yield her prey entirely. Nothing more remained but to consolidate the lightening belt and tow the unfortunate wreck back to Piraeus, after having recovered the corpses contained in her flanks.

Naturally, it was Poulpiquet who took responsibility for that sad exploration. Before working at a shallow depth he put on an ordinary diving-suit, which gave his limbs a greater freedom of movement. Then, equipped with a submarine electric lamp, a lever and pliers, he went down to the lower deck, after receiving minute instructions from the officers of the *Sirius* as to the exact location of the hatch to the third watertight compartment.

On the lower deck, nothing had budged. He could still see rolled-up hammocks fixed above his head. He walked over various utensils, plates and battered iron trays, a watch-team having been caught by the catastrophe while having a meal. He found the hatchway easily, hermetically sealed thanks to its rubber joints. With the aid of his lever he succeeded in shifting the bolts, already rusted by their sojourn in the water, and opened the entrance to the compartment. The ladder was still there and he was able to penetrate the fatal prison.

With the aid of his submarine lamp, he explored the sinister space with his gaze. The sight was terrifying. Everything was in a state of indescribable disorder, impossible to explain by the shipwreck alone. There was a tangle of broken crates, staved-in barrels and splintered planks, all heaped up in front of the square hole that had caused him so much surprise the previous day.

On pushing his research further, the bold diver perceived that the most distant parts of the room had suffered the least. He set about trying to discover the three bodies, but all his efforts were fruitless; he thought that, during the disaster, the unfortunate trio must have been buried by the displaced cargo, and were doubtless lying under heaps of barrels and bales. He went back up, and informed Sir Owen of the negative result of his first investigation.

After having rested for a little while, he went back down with two comrades.

After six trips, they had visited every inch, and had acquired the improbably certainty that the three missing men of the *Sirius* were no longer in the prison where they had been immured.

Then Poulpiquet, after first having cleared the vicinity of the square opening, examined it, and recognized without any possible mistake that it had been made by human hands. If any doubt had remained, they would have vanished when he found two files, chipped and worn, next to the hole. He brought them to the surface, along with one of several cylinders that he had noticed because they had been symmetrically arranged in a corner.

On the bridge of the *Investigator*, Sir Owen and all the senior officers were waiting anxiously.

"Well?" said he Englishman.

"Well, Commandant, there's no point in searching any longer for the bodies of Monsieur de Malher and his companions. We won't find them aboard the *Sirius*."

"Why not?"

"Because they got out."

"What do you mean?"

"Got out—yes, through the square opening I mentioned; an opening they made with these." He held out the files to Sir Owen.

"But that's impossible! They wouldn't have had time!"

"They got out, Commandant, and, in consequence, drowned."

"But how did they breathe while they were preparing that terrible escape attempt?"

"I don't know, but they did it."

Sir Owen's gaze then fell upon the cylinder that Poulpiquet had brought. He examined it, and red on a brass label the exergue: *Compagnie franco-hellénique de l'oxygène comprimé*. Those words provoked a flash of enlightenment. He remained pensive momentarily, and then, sadly, turned to the officers surrounding him.

"Messieurs," he said, "Poulpiquet is right. We'll never find our unfortunate friends, for only the sea can return them to us now. In the cargo destined for the cholera victims of Beyrouth, the *Sirius* was carrying compressed oxygen. Locked in that frightful grave, the prisoners owed a few hours respite to that oxygen. They must have been unable to bear the idea of waiting passively for death, and, brave men that they were, perhaps thinking that they were in relatively shallow water, they resolved to continue the struggle until the end. They employed the last hours of their existence in disputing the slow death that awaited them by means of a desperate effort. The depth at which the *Sirius* lay thwarted that heroic endeavor. Our brothers died like valiant men and Christians! God will have their souls, and the great tomb of mariners will keep their bodies."

Those words were spoken in a penetrating tone, in the midst of a religious silence on the part of the audience, who were reliving within themselves the anguish of the supreme struggle sustained by the victims of the *Sirius*. The ensign who had been in command of the vessel at the moment of the collision bit his lip until the blood flowed in order not to weep, and large tears flowed from poor Poulpiquet's eyes down the coarse wet fabric of his diving-suit.

PART TWO
THE SUBMARINE CITY

I
The Black Hole

For three days, the prisoners of the *Sirius* had been confined in their dangerous dungeon. They had gradually become accustomed to the permanent peril that threatened them, and applied themselves with an easily comprehensible ardor but also with a perfect self-composure to the preparations for their salvation. As true mariners, they had organized their existence rigorously. The hours of rest were strictly regulated, in such a way that two of them were awake while the third slept.

Meal-times were similarly fixed, and were, in any case, brief, for life in that enclosed space was not made to develop the appetite. The doctor was determined that they should be substantial, however, and especially that the menu should vary—which was easy enough, given the quantity and diversity of the canned goods appropriated from the larder. Several times, in fact, in order to overcome the disinclination of his companions, he had recourse to Halgouët's culinary talents; like every good matelot, the latter had some notion of the art of Carême. The laboratory retorts were set aside momentarily, and Quosé strove to produce a hot dish, which he baptized

113

with a name appropriate to the occasion: "tinned tongue *à la fond du cale*" or "deep-sea diver's corned beef." It was all washed down with a bottle generally decorated with the name of "Château-du-Fond" or "Clos-Marsouin."

He said to Georges de Malher: "Eat well, Commandant, or the Doctor will order you to take three hours' exercise on the deck every day…and I can assure you that it won't do you good."

The worthy fellow's constant good humor, and his absolute confidence in their success, reacted on the other two prisoners in spite of everything, and contributed more than a little to keeping their spirits up.

The manufacture of oxygen went well; it was, in any case, quite simple, merely a matter of heating potassium chlorate in a retort. In spite of the small dimensions of the alcohol lamp and the distillation apparatus, however, the difficulty lay in regulating the temperature. The doctor had succeeded in doing that, as he had announced, by means of an oxygen jet delivered through rubber tubing and projected into the flame by a nozzle made of zinc taken from the lining of the crates. In truth, the zinc melted quite rapidly, but they only had to replace it and, thank God, there was no shortage of the metal.

When all the reservoirs devoted to the oxygen were full, the doctor distilled sea-water trickling through the slender fissure that he had let alone. That distilled water was then stirred to aerate it, and served for both drinking and washing—for the most scrupulous hygiene was observed by the little colony. Frequent ablutions of fresh water rendered the body more comfortable and played a considerable role in the maintenance of health.

Finally, the doctor also obtained hydrogen, without difficulty, from the decomposition of water under the action of sulfuric acid and zinc, and he had soon filled the cylinders reserved specifically for that purpose.

While he was occupied with his retorts, his companions did not remain inactive. Halgouët fabricated the lifebelts and respiratory bags out of the rubberized cloth. He had no scissors, but he still had his matelot's knife, a strong blade of good steel, which he rendered as trenchant as a razor by sharpening it with an iron bar, and with its aid he cut the cloth very dexterously, stretched over the lid of a crate. He also made a spindle and a distaff, and after two hours' practice he was able, recalling the memories of his childhood, to fabricate with the oakum, combed with the aid of nails, a rather coarse but very resistant thread.

When Quosé was tired of cutting, he installed himself for spinning, crouching on a pile of barrels, his legs folded under him like a tailor. The two officers could not help laughing on seeing the gravity with which he devoted himself to that feminine task.

As for Georges de Malher, he had assumed the task of preparing "the exit door," as the doctor called it, by virtue of an amiable euphemism. He began by drawing a square fifty centimeters square on the sheet metal between two struts. Then he set up a powerful stay against the section that was to be blown out, formed by a piece of wood braced on the floor, destined to the pressure of the water that the filed sheet-metal might be impotent to support unaided. After that, he began the extraordinarily patient labor that consisted of hollowing out with the file, along the four marked sides, a groove about eight millimeters deep.

The work was atrociously tiring, by virtue of the inclined position that he was obliged to maintain and the smallness of the tools. There was also another obstacle to overcome; the files, continuously under pressure from the commencement of the operation, were soon worn down. That was serious, for if he did not succeeded in preparing the opening that the explosion was to complete, it would be necessary to renounce all hope.

The doctor, however, with the debris of the fencing foils, indented along their edges and tempered, fabricated a whole arsenal of tools that permitted him to work relentlessly without putting the files out of service. With the same materials he made chisels, which, struck with a hammer, chipped away tiny pieces of metal quite easily. From time to time, Quosé came to relieve the Commandant. The doctor sometimes helped out too—with the result that the groove became evident, and they were able to anticipate its completion within the time allotted.

One day—the sixth after the shipwreck—Quosé, who had been spinning for two hours, put down his distaff and addressed Sergeant.

"Doctor," he said, "I have nothing more to do. All my belts have been cut, my bags prepared, and here's a reel that ought to contain three hundred meters of thread. I think that's sufficient. So, would you like to assign me more work? Otherwise, I'll be obliged, regretfully to go in search of a new employer."

At that moment, Georges de Malher set down the implement that he was using and said: "I too, my dear Doctor, have completed my task. My groove has the required eight-millimeter depth along its entire length.

"Well, my friends," said the Doctor, who had just finished filling several food-tins with white powder, I've finished too. We have oxygen for at least two days, and

116

sufficient quantities of hydrogen to fill our belts—and I've just finished manufacturing the explosive that is going to open the door for us. Now it only remains to sew up our equipment and make the seams impermeable. Here are sufficient needles, which I've made from sharpened iron wire and tempered. As for the impermeable varnish, in accordance with the idea Quosé gave me, I'll manufacture carbon disulfide, in which we'll dissolve the debris of the rubberized fabric that Halgouët has set aside, and a few pieces of rubber tube."

"Here they are," said the matelot, indicating a heap of rags.

"Good. As they won't be enough, and we still have more impermeable cloth, we'll combine that debris with bits of fabric cut into small pieces. All the rubber will dissolve in the nauseating liquid, and we'll obtain an excellent varnish. We'll apply several layers of it to the seams; the carbon disulfide solution will evaporate, and only the rubber will remain on the safety-apparatus. It's going to smell very bad in here, though."

"Bah!" said Halgouët. "Our imprisonment will be coming to an end..."

"But my dear friend," the Commandant interjected, "are you sure you have what you need to manufacture carbon disulfide?"

"Certainly. We have several barrels of sulfur, which I brought for the purpose of fumigation."

"And carbon?"

"Carbon too. It's choice charcoal, passed through a sieve, broken up into tiny pieces of near-uniform size, which was to be used to make filters. So it isn't in sacks, but in boxes. We'll find them in a matter of minutes."

The three men started searching. After a hour, however, having examined everything, it was necessary to yield to the evidence: there was no charcoal in the compartment.

"Damn!" said Halgouët. "No charcoal, no carbon disulfide, no varnish. No varnish, no belts, and no belts..."

"Oh, shut up, Halgouët," said the doctor. "It's impossible for us to fail for want of a few sticks of charcoal. Let's search again."

They recommenced the investigations. They opened all the crates of whose contents they were not absolutely sure. They even searched the barrels. They found sulfur, but no trace of charcoal. For the first time, the doctor began to lose his composure. What he was experiencing was more than despair; it was anger—the anger of an energetic man who has calculated everything, planned everything, and yet cannot get as far as the end of the struggle because of an absurd, infinitely petty obstacle that surges forth at the last moment: the anger of an admiral who loses as battle because a signal has been misinterpreted, a general beaten because the powder in his cartridges his damp, or a financier ruined because a telegraph operator was playing billiards instead of picking up a dispatch.

"Come on," said the Commandant, "Don't abandon us, my friend. Thus far, you've incarnated all hope, confidence and courage for us! There must be other substances that dissolve rubber."

"Undoubtedly, but I no longer remember what they are. It's been twenty years since I occupied myself with rubber. And besides, will we have those substances? Will we possess what we need to manufacture them? Whereas, for carbon disulfide, I was so sure..."

"Keep looking, in spite of everything, my friend. I have an idea that Heaven won't abandon us."

"So it's you now who are maintaining my morale! All the same, it's terrible. To have succeeded in staying alive for a week in a submerged pontoon, preparing the most audacious escape that anyone has ever dared imagine, perhaps glimpsing salvation, or, at any rate, the great final battle, and to realize that it will doubtless be necessary for us to die anyway, without defending ourselves…!"

The doctor was pacing back and forth in the narrow space like a caged animal.

"Sergeant, my friend, calm down!"

"Come on, Doctor," said Halgouët, "We've overcome other obstacles. I'm sure you'll find the answer. Do you know what I think? I think we should start sewing, as if we were absolute sure of being able to apply the saving varnish to our seams."

"Yes, you're right, my poor friends," Sergeant replied. "But I've just experienced the greatest disappointment of my life."

"After that of not having seen cholera, of course," said Quosé, phlegmatically.

Once again, the worthy fellow succeeded in bringing a smile to his companions' lips.

The day passed sadly. The meals were bleak, in spite of the efforts Quosé put into them. Throughout the first half of the day the doctor worked silently with the Commandant and Halgouët. The three men were seated on barrels around a table formed by the huge lid of a crate nailed on to a larger barrel. Instead of the thimbles necessary to traverse the tough fabric with coarse and uneven needles, they had finger-guards of thick leather made from Halgouët's belt.

They were illuminated by a little spirit lamp set up by the doctor in a tin. Normally, it would only have provided a humble blue-tinted flame, but in this instance the oxygen intervened again. A thin stream of the gas was directed to the wick, which thus produced a bright glare. The apparatus was fixed, illuminating the desired part of the room by means of a reflector made with anther food-tin whose cylinder had been opened up, the interior of which was as shiny as silver. The lantern only served as a portable source of illumination now, and was rarely lit.

At five o'clock, the doctor stopped sewing. "Forgive me, my friends," he said, "but I'm incapable of sitting still. I'll rack my brains while I move around. I don't know whether it's the chagrin I'm experiencing, but I feel a kind of fatigue."

"If you were to have some cordial..."

"No thanks; it will pass if I can take a few steps."

"Calm down, Sergeant, I beg you," said Georges. "Seek tranquilly—you'll find it, I'm certain."

"You can see that I'm perfectly calm," relied the doctor brusquely. At the same time, he stamped his foot.

Georges and Halgouët looked at him anxiously. Sergeant resumed walking. From time to time he took out a little book, in which he had once made his notes. He hoped that by some impossible stroke of luck, there might be a providential indication made a long time ago in the book that he had carried on his person for years. Every time he put it back in his pocket, he took it out again, in case a few pages might perhaps have escaped his notice.

Suddenly, he stopped, put his hand to his head, and tottered. Halgouët, who was beside him, only just had time to catch him in his arms. Aided by the Commandant, he laid him down on one of the rudimentary bunks on which they spent their brief periods of repose.

"Oh, my God!" said the Breton. "Poor fellow! What's happened to him?"

Georges felt his pulse. Like all men in charge of others, whose profession exposes them frequently to spending time in collaboration with practitioners of the art, he had a smattering of medical knowledge.

"The pulse is slightly weak," he said, "but regular. I don't think it's anything serious. Where's the first aid kit?"

"Here."

Georges opened it, took out a bottle of ether, and made his friend breathe it in. At the same time, Halgouët forced a few drops of rum between his clenched teeth. The effect was swift. After five minutes, Sergeant opened his eyes. He remained seemingly dazed for a moment or two, and then said: "Oh, is it my turn on watch? You must have had difficulty waking me. I was sleeping deeply, wasn't I? I have a headache."

"Do you want to go back to sleep?"

"No, no, it's my turn..." Sergeant recovered his sense of reality completely. "But in fact," he said, "I wasn't asleep...I fainted, stupidly, like a Marquise. Isn't that stupid?"

"It's the mental torture, the ardent research, and the terrible effort you've been making this morning, my poor comrade."

"Yes...and the disappointment. But I'll be better. A little water to dampen my temples, and it'll be gone."

While Halgouët brought him the water in a mug, the doctor sat up. "What's that smell?" he asked, suddenly.

"Ether, We made you breathe it in."

"Oh, that's true...but my friends...oh, my friends...!"

The doctor stood up abruptly, his eyes almost haggard.

"What is it, Doctor? What?" exclaimed Jean and Georges, alarmed once again.

"My friends, ether also dissolves rubber!"

The three men exchanged a vigorous embrace, and tears rose to their eyes.

"You see," said Georges. "God hasn't abandoned us! But you need to get completely better, my friend. We need you."

"Oh, I'm better—totally. Joy is the best of remedies, my lads."

"Pardon me, Doctor," said Jean, with a residue of anxiety, "but there isn't much ether."

"I know, my friend—but I have what I need to manufacture ether, and this time, I'm sure. Hand me the alcohol and the sulfuric acid...good. Now bring me the expended lime. I need sand to make a kind of basin, but as I don't have any, we'll use the lime. That's it. Now direct the oxygen at the alcohol burner. In forty-eight hours, we'll be out of the *Sirius*!"

Two days later, the final preparations were complete. Nothing more remained but to contrive the explosion.

With everything the compartment contained by way of boxes, planks and barrels, they built a kind of rampart around the panel that was to be blown out. The doctor fitted the cartridge to the delineated square, compounded as carefully as possible so as not to exceed the required effect. The ignition was to be provided by an impact. To obtain the impact they had suspended a heavy mass by a cord that ended in a fuse. By setting fire to the fuse, the flame would spread to the cord, whose combustion would determine the fall of the mass, and, in consequence, the explosion.

Naked to the waist, clad in their apparatus, their mouths applied to the respirators, the three men retreated into the depths of the compartment, after having clear the space necessary to reach the opening without encountering any obstacle. A strong cable extended to the place where the ship would open up would serve to assist and guide them.

It had been agreed that Halgouët, the matelot, would pass through first; that Sergeant, the officer, would go second, and that Georges, the Commandant, would be the last.

When everything was ready, the doctor lit the fuse.

Then the three of them, holding hands and reciting a mute prayer, they waited.

Scarcely a minute went by—but what a minute!

A terrible explosion burst. The heap of objects collapsed. The ship trembled. The three men were hurled to the floor, shaken by the blast, blinded by the smoke, but safe and sound.

They got up, clinging to the cable...

The water did not come in.

"That's strange!" Sergeant exclaimed. "You didn't dig deep enough, de Malher—the wall has held!"

The Commandant picked up the lantern, which, protected by its thick armature, had not gone out, ran to the wall and uttered a cry of astonishment.

"What is it? What is it?"

"The wall hasn't held. The ship is holed."

"What can you see, then?"

"I can see a black hole—and air is coming through the hole!"

II
Into the Unknown

Nothing can give any idea of the surprise that the Commandant's exclamation provoked in his two companions. In two bounds they joined him, and examined by the light of the lantern the singular breach through which water ought to be flooding, but through which air was penetrating: damp air, impregnated with the odor of a cellar, but air nevertheless.

They observed that the hollowed-out wall had blown out in accordance with the excavated grooves, but the sliced sheet metal was not the only thing forming the edges of the opening; beyond it there was a mattress of clay, against which the flank of the *Sirius* had been laying. Beneath that mattress there was a crust of light and friable stone, somewhat analogous to pumice-stone but much denser. The explosion had staved in the clay and broken through the stony crust.

A few drops of water were filtering between the ship and the clay. It was easy to anticipate that at the slightest displacement of the vessel, which was now serving, relative to the black hole, the function of a gigantic lid, the water would gush into the cavity that had thus been opened up.

The result they had obtained was so unexpected, so contrary to all their anticipations, that the three men, still dazed by the commotion of the explosion, stood their momentarily, as if deaf and dumb.

Georges de Malher was the first to recover full possession of himself. He tapped the doctor on the shoulder;

the latter, leaning against the wall, was letting the lantern hang down, trying to plumb the darkness of the cavern. "Come on, my friends," he said, "I don't think we have time to waste. We need to make a decision. The prow of the *Sirius* is obviously embedded in the sea-bed. It's possible that the starboard side isn't so deeply engaged, but that's not certain. Are we going to start our work over?"

"We couldn't, even if we wanted to," replied Sergeant. My apparatus has been partly shattered by the explosion; out tools are dispersed—and in any case, the hole we've opened up is a threat even more dangerous than everything else!"

"Then there's only one thing we can do. A door is open, air is coming through it. It must, therefore, communicate with a point situated above sea-level. The road by which we must seek deliverance is there, and it's the only one."

"Yes," said the doctor and Halgouët, simultaneously. "It's the only one."

"And with your permission," said Halgouët, "I'll go right away to reconnoiter the entrance to the tunnel. It ought to be me, as I'm the most agile."

"Yes, you go, Halgouët—but we'll help you."

The three prisoners took off the belts they had gone to such trouble to make, which were unnecessary henceforth. They picked up ropes, tied them together rapidly, and improvised a cable ten meters long, which Halgouët fitted it under his arms. The doctor and the Commandant wound it around one of the stanchions, and the intrepid Breton, lantern in hand, let himself down through the opening.

After a few moments, he shouted: "I'm at the bottom."

"Where are you?"

"In a kind of cave with vertical walls."

"How deep, approximately?

"About eight meters. I've got a kind of tunnel in front of me."

"How wide?"

"About two meters?"

"And high?"

"Quite high—I can't see the ceiling."

"Can you get in there?"

"Yes. I'll undo the rope."

Five minutes went by. Leaning over the edge of the hole, the two officers waited anxiously. It seemed to them that hours passed. Finally, they saw the lamp-light at the bottom of the well.

"Commandant!"

"Well?"

"I've taken fifty strides into the tunnel. The air goes a long way."

"Is the ground horizontal?"

"No, it slopes upwards.

"Much?"

"Oh yes, quite steeply."

"Good. Wait a minute Halgouët—there's no point in your coming back. We'll join you."

Addressing Georges, the doctor said: "The tunnel slopes upwards. It contains air. We only have to go down. It's a matter of reaching, if the slope continues, a level at which the sea can no longer get to us before it follows us along the same route. Let's only take the strict necessities: water, biscuit, and oil for the lamp."

The impermeable belts changed their function, one being transformed into a sack, the others to water-skins. They send them all down to Halgouët, who received

126

them at the bottom. Then the doctor picked up two iron bars that were close at hand. Finally, he did not forget the remainder of the explosives he had made, which might prove useful in disposing of some obstacle.

Less than half an hour after the explosion, the two officers slid down the cable and rejoined Jean Halgouët.

"My friends," said the Commandant, let's march quickly. We're in the unknown, but all things considered, it's better than the watertight compartment of the *Sirius*."

The shipwreck victims found themselves in a kind of vaulted grotto, broadly elliptical in form, the walls of which were formed of irregular layers of the friable but rather compact stone that the doctor had noticed at the orifice of the hole. The ground was strewn with debris fallen from the vault. Facing them was the entrance to the tunnel discovered by Halgouët. The three men went into it, walking at a rapid pace. Their situation was certainly as alarming as it had been the day before, but they experienced, without daring to communicate it to one another, a vague sentiment of hope. The natural air, stale as it was, which they were now breathing, which came from the free external atmosphere, seemed to increase their vital force, and there was a kind of gluttony in the way they filled their lungs with it.

In addition, they found in intense pleasure in marching freely, straight ahead, without being stopped every ten paces by an iron partition, and the sensation of reconquered movement gave them an extra measure of vigor. Then again, when one is undergoing such strange and difficult ordeals, any change seems to bring with it, even in the midst of a disquieting mystery, a relief and a hope. So the bold companions were able to apply the formula that often recurs in military bulletins and affirm that, although their situation was still perilous, at least their morale was excellent,

Halgouët marched in the lead carrying the lantern. They had covered some three hundred meters in the corridor, and the terrain was still rising at a steep slope, to the point that the climb, for men who had been confined in a dungeon for a week, was becoming difficult. They were obliged to pause momentarily to get their breath back.

"Anyway," said Halgouët, "where on earth can we be?"

That question responded exactly to the interior reflections of the Commandant and the doctor.

"In truth," said the later, "this isn't the time to discuss geology—but judging by the regularity of the walls of the tunnel that we're following, I believe that we're in some submarine grotto of volcanic origin. You know that basaltic caves often form pathways and chambers of an almost geometric configuration. Let's not forget that we're in the Greek archipelago—which is to say, one of the regions of the globe most tormented by the terrestrial fire."

The Commandant took the lantern from Halgouët's hand and projected the light on one of the lateral walls. It seemed to be made of large superimposed blocks, but whose joints had disappeared under lava-flows and calcareous efflorescences. Everywhere, under the influence of a penetrating damp and oozing water that was streaming over the walls, dampening the floor, the stone was becoming scaly and crumbling. The hypothesis offered by Sergeant seemed plausible to his companions, and as they did not have time to debate it, as the doctor had just said, they contented themselves with it and set off again.

It was still impossible to make out the ceiling that covered the strange path. As he walked, the Commandant picked up a pebble and threw it in the air. The stone collided with the ceiling after an appreciable interval; the tunnel had to be about ten meters deep. He repeated the experiment several times, and obtained the same result. He had just renewed it for the fourth time when Halgouët, who was still in the lead, stopped.

"Look," he said. "A doorway!"

"A doorway?"

"Exactly, and very correct!"

His two companions moved closer. The Breton was not mistaken. It really was a doorway; they could clearly make out its jutting jambs and its lintel, on which they could even make out a few traces of sculpture.

"My God, Doctor," said Halgouët, "you can think what you like, but for my part, I don't believe in the basalt anymore."

"Of course not!" replied Sergeant.

"It appears," said the Commandant, "That we're not yet at the end of our adventures."

"Well, after all," said the doctor, "if it's a doorway, let's go through it, and see what's on the other side."

"That's entirely indicated," said George de Malher. "Go, on, Halgouët."

On the other side, there was a kind of room that might have measured five or six meters on each side. To the right there was a second opening similar to the first. It was, therefore, necessary to cross the redoubt diagonally in order to reach it. But that new opening was pierced in a wall much thicker than the other. The explorers' first concern was to check that it was not a dead end. They counted nine paces, or about six meters, before emerging from the corridor it formed, and recognized that it ended at a rather large crossroads, where massive inexplicable constructions formed a kind of goose-foot, forming the intersection of several routes.

"There's no doubt about it," said the Commandant. "We're neither in a cave nor in some kind of undersea quarry. We're in a city."

"Yes," the doctor replied, "We're in a city, but why has this city, sunk beneath the level of the sea, not been inundated? That's what I can't explain."

"Nor me," said the Commandant.

"Nor me," added Halgouët, and added: "But if you want more precise information, I can give it to you, thanks to the lantern. Look at these sculptures that I'm illuminating in the two granite jambs of the doorway."

The companions drew nearer. The hard pink granite had resisted the action of time, and on the scarcely-unpolished faces of the jambs it was easy to make out two figures: two stiff humans whose bodies were face-on and whose heads were in profile. Each of them was holding a square shield in one hand and a bow and arrows in the other. Their eyes, designed as complex almost-shapes in spite of the profile, their coiffure, reminiscent of a sphinx, and their loincloths left no doubt as to the origin of the sculptures.

"That's decisive," said Sergeant. "We're in an Egyptian city."

"That's obvious," replied Georges de Malher. "Look how the door-jambs widen out toward the base."

"And that lintel, which presents a bulging form, with a string of lotus leaves," Halgouët added.

The Commandant and the doctor looked at one another in surprise on hearing that reflection formulated in the simplest manner by the Breton.

"So, my dear comrade," said Georges, "you know something about Egyptian architecture?"

"Yes, a little. I could tell you things that would make you die laughing if we weren't so busy. The captain who educated me knew a lot about it, and he took it into his head to inculcate me with a little of his science. I'll be hanged, though, if I ever thought it might help me one day to get my bearings, so to speak."

"Well," said the Commandant, "it seems that popular legends aren't always as childish as one is led to believe."

"To what legend are you alluding?"

"The one that's current in the nearby island of the archipelago, which says that the islet of Syrtos is only the last vestige of a much larger island, inhabited by an Egyptian colony, which was buried under the sea, many centuries before our era, after an eruption."

"As happened in 1862 to the island of Santorini," said Sergeant.

"Precisely."

"The legend is obviously not mistaken, and we're in the ancient city of Syrta. But I'll return to our question of a little while ago: that the city was buried under sea level by the lowering of the ground is natural and explicable—but that it wasn't inundated, I can't understand."

"Perhaps we'll have the key to the mystery later. For the moment, we need to go on. We have three routes in front of us; which one shall we take?"

"My God," said Quosé, "I'm no great scholar, but it seems to me that we ought to take the one that slopes upwards the most."

"Good sense suggests that—except that a road can go up only to descend again thereafter. I think we should explore all three of the roads facing us for a certain distance."

"What about light?" asked the Breton.

"We'll make it as we go," the doctor replied. Does the lantern have a long wick?"

"Not very."

"Well then, we'll braid some pieces of cloth and make two lamps with two wrought iron mugs."

"I only have one."

"Damn! If we can only explore two routes, we'll lose time."

"Don't worry, Doctor," said Quosé. "A lamp-lighter of the time of the pharaohs has doubtless anticipated our visit, for he's left lighting equipment to hand, ready for use." While speaking, the matelot picked an antique bronze lamp shaped like a duck's head out of a kind of niche situated to the right of the doorway.

"It's a guard-room lamp," he said.

"A guard-room?"

"Yes. The long tunnel we've been following thus far is the space separating the double wall circling the city. The Egyptians, who had their own ideas about fortification and liked simple methods, didn't dig ditches, but they made two walls. To penetrate their citadels, they fitted chambers between the two walls whose doors weren't in the same alignment. We've just come through one of those redoubts. Finally, the two soldiers sculpted there inform us as to the function of the building we've just emerged from. Let's pour some oil into this duck's-head, Doctor, and add a wick to it. It's not every day one has the opportunity to light one's way in an Egyptian city with a lamp three thousand years old."

The three men separated, and agreed to meet up against at the "archers' door."

"Above all," Georges recommended to his two companions, "don't go into any bifurcation, any lateral route. Just take note of the direction and the slope, and the chances we have of finding the way clear."

Twenty minutes later, the Doctor, who had followed the middle way, returned to the rendezvous first. He was almost immediately joined by Quosé, who had taken the route to the right.

"Well?" said Sergeant.

"Well, the route I was following went downwards."

"Mine too, but I arrived at another intersection, and didn't want to go any further."

"I was stopped by a collapse after two hundred paces—impossible to go any further.

At that moment, Georges de Malher returned. He had been luckier than his companions; the route he had followed formed a long curve, but after two or three hundred meters, traveled amid rubble, he had observed that the ground was still rising. Furthermore, he had the conviction of having eventually breathed in fresher air; he even thought that he had sensed a momentary current.

They did not hesitate. The three men took the left-hand route, and, walking with difficulty over the rubble with which the floor was strewn, breathless and streaming with sweat, but with hope in their hearts, they filed before the terrifying and bleak eyes of a huge granite sphinx, crouching like a beast of prey with its legs outstretched, which stared at them.

II
An Article in the Agora

As soon as Sir Owen, following the reflotation of the *Sirius*, had acquired the certainty that the cadavers of the victims would not be found aboard the unfortunate ship, he left the Investigator where she was and returned to Piraeus aboard one of the steamers he had chartered to serve as auxiliaries. He had given his second-in-command the instructions necessary to complete the flotation and put the *Sirius* into a state to be towed. His presence was unnecessary in the waters off the islet of Syrtos, and imperious duties recalled him to Greece.

First of all, he was very anxious at not having seen Madame de Malher arrive, her advent having been announced as so imminent at the moment of his departure that he had, as will be remembered, prepared a steamship for her usage, the *Militiade*.

Secondly, he had placed the matelot Thomas Tingle, the author of the *Sirius* disaster, in the hands of the maritime authorities. He was the most important witness of the matelot's criminal action, and, to a certain extent, as commander of the *Investigator*, he shared the moral responsibility with him.

Finally, Sir Owen, wanted to make the necessary arrangements, without delay, for the erection of a durable monument to the memory of the unfortunate compatriots on the deserted islet near to which the terrible maritime drama had unfolded.

On arrival at Pireaus, he realized that he had done well to hurry.

To begin with, he learned that his niece, severely tested by the unexpected news of the catastrophe that had rendered her a widow, had fallen ill during her dolorous journey, and had been obliged to take to bed in Vienna. For two days the poor young woman had been battling the affliction of a cerebral congestion that had almost carried her of. The danger was now averted, but the invalid's condition necessitated great care, and it was necessary above all to contend with the obsession that she had of escaping the care with which one of her relatives, altered by telegraph, was surrounding her and hastened to the site of the disaster. By virtue of a strange conception of the delirium of the fever, Madame de Malher was crying out repeatedly that her husband was alive, that no one knew where to find him, and that she alone could save him.

One can imagine how this bad news added to Sir Owen's chagrin, but other emotions still awaited him.

Thomas Tingle, at the request of the English consul, had been locked up in a jail appended to the maritime authority of Piraeus, pending the arrival of the English ironclad cruiser *Nelson*. Under the terms of maritime law, the guilty party had, in fact, to be judged by a court martial convened either in the English base nearest to the scene of the crime or aboard a warship of the British navy. As the *Nelson* had been due to call at Piraeus, it had been decided to keep the prisoner until the ship was in the harbor, and then to put him at the disposal of its captain.

Now, when Sir Owen arrived, the English ironclad had been moored since the day before. The sailor had immediately been moved aboard and put in irons, and the captain had announced a date for the court martial to the recorder charged with the investigation.

In all countries, the essential character of military justice is its rapidity, so Sir Owen was not surprised to receive, as soon as he disembarked, a summons inviting him to appear before the reporter without delay, aboard the *Nelson*, not only in the capacity of witness but also "to answer, if necessary, as captain of the *Investigator*, for the ramming of the *Sirius* by his ship." The unfortunate scientist had passed, without any possible doubt, to the rank of accused.

The affair, as one can imagine, was making a great deal of noise, principally in the foreign colony. The French, in spite of what was known about Sir Owen's upright and generous character, were guarding a tenacious rancor against him. In the circles where his compatriots gathered, as well as the dining-tables in the hotels, people were discussing at great length the "famous English theory that consists of regarding all the seas as the property of the United Kingdom and riding roughshod over insolent individuals who allow themselves to navigate there."

In vain, moderate minds remarked that the owner of the *Investigator* was making every possible effort to repair the damage he had caused. In vain, they described the dolor experienced by the worthy gentleman. The current was too strong. And when Sir Owen passed, absorbed and busy, through the streets of Athens or Pireaus, he would have been able to remark, had he been less preoccupied, the hostile glances that the Frenchmen whose paths he crossed were casting at him.

Several times, in fact, he was forced to perceive, in spite of himself, the sentiments that he provoked. Thus, going into a shop one day, he saw a whole group of customers make their exit with affectation without completing their purchases. Too just not to excuse such resentment, and too sure of his conscience to feel diminished by it, he supported the insult stoically. But he experienced a sharp pain, which his self-control was scarcely sufficient to conceal.

He did not, in fact, even have the resource of regaining strength in the company of his compatriots, many of who held against him the evil renown cast on their fatherland, and willingly allowed themselves, in ignorance of the true facts, to accuse him at the least of inexperience and incapacity. Thus, Sir Owen wished with all his heart that the day of judgment would arrive.

For his part, the captain of the *Nelson* wanted to get the annoying affair over and done with as soon as possible. The investigation was rapidly completed. Someone was sent to Syrtos in quest of the mariners of the *Investigator* whose testimony might clarify the affair, and three days after the *Nelson*'s arrival in Piraeus, the court martial was in session.

This is the translation of the article in the Greek newspaper, the *Agora*, giving an account of the hearing in question:

A MARITIME CRIME
The Ramming and Sinking of the French ship *Sirius*

Yesterday, aboard the armored cruiser *Nelson*, the judgment took place of the two persons accused of causing the sinking of the French naval vessel *Sirius*, which was traveling in all haste to Beyrouth to bring aid to the population, ravaged by cholera. It is on an order sent expressly from London by the Admiralty that the court martial has been convened aboard the *Nelson*. The Admiralty, in fact, in view of the circumstances in which the crime was committed, has deemed that the repression must be immediate, and the special missions confided by it to Sir Owen Townsend, captain of the *Investigator*, give it an official character that render him and his crew, without any possible contest, answerable to the jurisdiction of the British Ministry of War.

The court martial is comprised by Captain Taylor, presiding, a frigate captain, two lieutenants, two second lieutenants and a non-commissioned officer. The functions of recording magistrate are fulfilled by a lieutenant first-class, those of the government commissioner and clerk by two administrative officers.

The court martial meets on the poop deck of the *Nelson*, under cover of a large tent. A table covered with green baize has been set up. Behind it, chairs await the judges. To the left and the right are two smaller tables, one for the clerk and the other for the government commissioner, and in front of the latter, two chairs for the accused. In the middle of the main table there is a Bible on which the witnesses will take the oath. Armed marine fusiliers outline a clear space closed at its extremity by a cable extended from one gunwale to the other.

It is impossible to imagine a décor simpler, and yet more imposing, than that improvised courtroom, dominated to either side by the iron turrets in which gigantic cannon are dormant, and closed at the back by the broad red pleats of the British flag, which flutters in the breeze and causes the mast to which it is attached to quiver by virtue of the tension in its halyard.

The hearing being public, some fifty men belonging to the *Nelson*'s crew are gathered behind the cable. Complete silence reigns, the military silence born of respect for discipline. Behind the seat reserved for the tribunal, thirty chairs have been set out for a few officers of the Greek navy, the French and English consuls, a number of our magistrates and the representatives of the press, to whom Captain Taylor has courteously given permission to follow the debates.

At noon precisely, a command rings out. The guard presents arms, the court takes its place round the table, and the guests, who have thus far been grouped in rear, sit down in the prepared seats. Captain Taylor, an old white-haired mariner with a clear and frank gaze, gives the order to bring in the accused.

During the brief interval separating that order from its execution, we look at the tribunal. All the officers comprising it are in full dress uniform. They strive to remain impassive, but beneath the cold masks they impose upon themselves, by the very reason of that attitude, too obviously contrived, one senses the penetration of a sentiment of sadness and a kind of humiliation in judging, under foreign eyes, compatriots who have compromised the honor of the flag.

Suddenly, there is a stir; a man of middle age, tall and upright, clad in a formal frock-coat with gray gloves, cleaves through the crowd of sailors gathered behind the cable. He advances into the empty space, hat in hand, arrives three paces in front of the table, bows to the tribunal, and goes to sit down in one of the chairs reserved for the accused. It is Sir Owen Townsend, the owner and captain of the *Investigator*, who has been summoned at liberty.

Almost at the same time, the second accused makes his entrance, between two sailors with sabers in hand. Thomas Tingle is a robust individual with a red face and a russet beard. He walks with a heavy tread, waddling from one leg to the other, bracing himself on the deck at every step, as if he fears that it might pitch. He too salutes the tribunal, militarily, and then goes to sit down on the second chair. One notices then that, with an instinctive movement, Sir Owen moves his own chair away, and turns his back on his co-accused. Behind Thomas Tingle a midshipman comes forward, who is to present his defense. Sir Owen has declared that he will do without the assistance of a defender.

The president declares the session open, and proceeds immediately with the initial formalities. Sir Owen declares his name and qualities thus: "Townsend, Richard Owen, baronet, member of the Royal Society of London, naturalist, certified long-haul captain, commander of the yacht *Investigator*, aged fifty-one years."

The sailor gets up in his turn and announces the following identification: "Tingle, Thomas James, former first-class seaman in the Royal Navy, presently hired seaman aboard the *Investigator*, aged thirty-one years."

The clerk reads the charge-sheet. Our readers know the facts already from our previous articles, so there is no need to transcribe that document. The sole point to remember is that, after the ramming of the *Sirius*, the captain of the *Investigator* laid s formal charge against Thomas Tingle, and that it is solely in his capacity as the commander of the ship that carried out the ramming that he has been brought before the court martial, as being responsible for the disaster until proven otherwise.

The charge-sheet, affirmative as regards the sailor, is less harsh with regard to the captain, but it nevertheless incriminates him clearly by attributing the disaster to his negligence.

After the reading of that document, the president begins the interrogations, commencing with Sir Owen. The latter replies to the questions in a grave and sad voice, without circumlocutions, limiting himself to establishing the reality of the facts. He states that he took all the precautions recommended by maritime regulations for navigation in fog, and remarks that, when he summoned Thomas Tingle to the helm in the fog, it was precisely because the sailor was a former seaman first class in the Royal Navy, who had spent three years as helmsman on Her Majesty's ships, and who seemed in consequence to be more experienced than any other.

The president then passes on to the interrogation of Thomas Tingle. The sailor's defense at least has the merit of simplicity. The accused, in fact, declares that he was mistaken and misunderstood the captain's order. It was by mistake that he turned the helm hard to port when he ought to have steered to starboard. One senses that he has been schooled by his defender, who, obliged to sustain a bad case, has tried to put it in the best possible light.

Unfortunately, the witnesses give the lie to Tingle in no uncertain terms. First of all, there are notes relative to the aptitude of the accused and notes relative to his record, which the president has read. It results from those indications that Tingle is an excellent helmsman, who has given real proof of composure on several occasions. On the other hand, they represent him as quarrelsome, and mention, among other disciplinary punishments, a considerable number of days in irons imposed at different times after brawls, principally with French mariners.

Then comes an able seaman from the *Investigator*, who, perched on the foot-step at the base of the yacht's main-mast shortly before the collision in order to adjust a halyard, witnessed the entire scene, and was one of the first to run to lend a hand to the captain when the latter ordered the arrest of the helmsman.

Finally, there are the mariners from the English yacht who, on the eve of the ship's departure, witnessed a quarrel between Tingle and a mariner from the *Sirius* in a tavern in Piraeus, and had heard their comrade swear that he would seize the first opportunity offered to him to sink a French ship. All those worthy men arrived, one after another, very sad to have to accuse a comrade; they remained silent before the court martial, twisting their berets in their rough hands. Then, when the rough hand in question was placed on the Bible, and they swore to tell the truth, they spoke, some experiencing a need to excuse themselves with regard to the sailor.

"You know, Tingle, that it pains me a great deal to say what I'm saying, but it's the truth, poor fellow...and I've sworn to tell it."

Tingle then shrugged his shoulders and replied: "All that doesn't prove that I wasn't mistaken in taking starboard for port."

After the witness statements, the government commissioner presents his speech for the prosecution. The honorable officer declares that Thomas Tingle was obviously the author responsible for the catastrophe, and that he acted, without any possible doubt, with premeditation. His crime, established by all the witnesses, is assimilable to the most characteristic acts of piracy.

According to the government commissioner, however, the responsibility of Thomas Tingle does not obliterate that of the captain. The latter, in fact, is morally responsible for the choice of his men and, even taking into account the difficulty of continued surveillance of the observation of all orders given, he ought to have taken measures to ensure that, in default of himself, one of his officers was making sure that his commands were scrupulously carried out. The commissioner draws the attention of the tribunal to the opprobrium cast on the flag by such a crime, and esteems that the severe punishment awaiting a simple seamen will be insufficient to wash it away. In consequence, he demands the death penalty for Thomas Tingle, and leaves it to the wisdom of the tribunal to inflict a penalty on the captain of the *Investigator* that, in showing that all England reproves such actions severely, will give satisfaction to the public conscience.

Sir Owen had listened with the greatest composure to the speech for the prosecution. When the officer had finished, he waited calmly for the president to invite him to speak. We transcribe his response, which was brief, in full:

"Gentlemen, I am not here to defend myself. I do not believe that the public conscience, any more than the honor of the flag, demands any other condemnation that that of the guilty party. Now, the guilty party is the seaman Thomas Tingle. No one will do me the insult of believing that I am avoiding a responsibility by putting the blame on a subaltern. I am no more now than on the day after the catastrophe a man who is defending himself. I am a man who is accusing, and who is accusing with conviction, because he knows, and because he has seen. I have presented myself before you out of respect for the laws of my country, and out of deference for the worthy gentlemen making up the tribunal. I have taken this chair because it was designated for me, but neither the placement of this chair nor my respect gives me the quality of an accused individual, which I repudiate with all my might.

"If I were accused, I do not know whether I could defend myself by charging a simple seaman. Not being accused, in my estimation, I remain simply the captain of the *Investigator*, who has done his duty entirely, who could not avoid an unworthy treason impossible to anticipate, and who, in the name of that same public conscience, in the name of the good renown of England, which the public minister invoked just now, is filing the dolorous but imperious duty of demanding the punishment of the traitor.

"I have nothing to add, Gentlemen. You are men of the sea, and you are just."

That curious speech, pronounced in a very clear voice, but somewhat vibrant with emotion, produced a profound impression on the audience. In spite of the impassivity of the judges, it was visible that that pride and that pretention justified a change of role, that disdain for a defense to which Sir Owen did not want even to descend, had not changed the convictions of the members of the court martial, convictions which must have been solidly founded already, but had given their sentiments their true and, so to speak, tangible formula.

The task of the young midshipman who had accepted to defend Thomas Tingle was difficult. He got out of it to his honor. First he apologized for having to put in doubt the convictions of a man like Sir Owen, and to be obliged to sustain that the captain of the *Investigator* might have been mistaken in attributing Tingle's action to a premeditated idea. According to him, the sailor had been guilty of one of those fatal errors, one of those unconscious aberrations that even the people most experienced in their métier cannot escape. He sincerely did not believe that hatred, even the most intense, could make an English seaman commit such a crime. But, even admitting that Tingle might have been obedient to such a sentiment, following the accusation on to its own terrain, he begged the court to consider that his client had an uncultivated nature, that he had often been provoked by the French, and that the sentiment that had guided him, if Tingle really was guilty was, in sum, a kind of deviation of patriotism. He counted, in consequence, on the clemency of the judges, and begged them, if they truly thought that a punishment was necessary, not to cut short the life of a man of thirty.

After that speech, the judges retired to deliberate. The session was resumed after scarcely ten minutes, and the president, standing up, as was the entire audience, read the judgment that acquitted Sir Owen Townsend and condemned Thomas Tingle to death.

The sailor shrugged his shoulders, turned to the guards and simple said: "All right. Let's go." And, passing in front of us in order to return to the ship's prison, he laughed loudly. "Thomas Tingle is going to be hanged," he said. "But he still drowned a few of *them*."

As for Sir Owen, he bowed to the tribunal, picked up his hat and headed for the vessel's exit port. As he went past, the naval officers nodded their heads, and it was observed that as he set foot on the first rung of the ladder, the French consul came to congratulate him and shake his hand.

Three days later, the newspapers from which we have borrowed the preceding account published the following short article:

EPILOGUE TO A MARITIME DRAMA
Execution of the Guilty Man

Yesterday morning the execution took place of Seaman Thomas Tingle, convicted of having deliberately and with premeditation having caused the sinking of the French naval vessel *Sirius*, and condemned to death by the court martial held aboard the *Nelson*.

On the advice of his defender, the wretch had, on the very evening of the verdict, entered his appeal. The appeal tribunal having been constituted by the captain of the *Nelson* at the same time as the court martial, the appeal could be examined the following day. As is well-known, appeals tribunals cannot pass judgment on the fundamental of the matter submitted to them. Their mission is limited to examining the procedure and establishing that the prescriptions of the law have been followed scrupulously. In the trial that concluded with the conviction of Thomas Tingle there could be no doubt. Captain Taylor was too experienced to have neglected any formality whatsoever. Thus, the tribunal had purely and simply confirmed the decision of the initial judges.

The execution did not take place in harbor. At daybreak, the Nelson set forth under low steam and put out to sea, with the aim of avoiding the manifestations of curiosity that would have been provoked by the action of justice had it been carried out in proximity to the city. No one was admitted to witness it. With a few colleagues of the Hellenic press and a few correspondents of foreign newspapers, however, we charted a tug that was able to remain within a short distance of the *Nelson*, which permitted us, thanks to excellent binoculars, to follow every detail of the tragic scene that unfolded aboard the English ironclad.

This is what we saw:

Having arrived six miles out to sea, the *Nelson* stops. The poop deck is completely deserted. The Guard, fully armed, lined up facing aft, forms a curtain on men barring entry to it completely. The master gunner arrives, who, aided by two men, passes a rope over a pulley attacked to the yardarm of the mizzen mast; he is followed by the purser, in service uniform, who is fulfilling the function of clerk and will shortly read the sentence to the condemned man, and a civilian dressed in a long black frock-coat, coifed in a small soft felt hat, with a book under his arm. The latter is the Reverend John Hardstone, the ship's chaplain. While he waits, he paces up and down the empty space, his chin on his hand, with a sad and meditative expression. After a few moments the commander of the guard approaches and talks to him. A few other officers come to join them.

It is nine o'clock. From out tug we can hear distinctly, in the calm air, the strokes of the *Nelson*'s sonorous bell. A command: the guard presents arms. At the same time, a group appears at the starboard staircase of the poop. It is the condemned man, bare-headed, his hands tied behind his back, climbing up escorted by four sailors with sabers in hand. So far as we can judge, he climbs the steep steps of the stairway without weakness, with a firm tread. He advances into the middle of the empty space. A battery of drums resounds briefly, opening the proclamation. The purser, with the government commissioner beside him, reads the sentence. We believe we can distinguish, through our binoculars, the tremor of the paper he is holding in his hand. The reading, very brief, is saluted at the end by a further rum roll, concluding the proclamation.

The four men guarding the condemned man draw apart then. The reverend approaches, exchanges a few words with Tingle, places the open Bible before his eyes and indicates verses to him with his finger. Then he bows to the sailor and retreats. The master gunner puts his hand on the patient's shoulder and leads him to the port shroud. He goes up first; Tingle follows, still without weakness—but with his hands bound, he cannot climb the ratlines without energetic assistance from the master gunner's aides. Arrived at mid-height, he stops. The rope is passed around his neck. A loud cry rings out, a hoarse but powerful clamor, in which we only recognize the word "Frenchmen"—doubtless a supreme invective, one last howl addressed to the French. Then the aides shove him into space with a vigorous thrust, and, almost without convulsion. The criminal's body swings from the yardarm of the vessel's mizzen mast.

Justice is done.

IV
The House of the Egyptian Goldsmith

The route taken by Georges de Malher and his companions was not easy. Scarcely had they passed the sphinx than they found themselves in a kind of narrow alleyway that must once have been three or four meters wide, but which ruins, heaped up everywhere, had shrunk considerably. The houses to either side of the street had been cracked, broken open and demolished. In places, the walls were no longer anything but heaps of rubble welded together by microscopic vegetation of which time had made a kind of cement.

Elsewhere, broad fissures opened in the walls, unmasking black and mysterious depths, from which a heavy and mephitic air escaped that caused the flames of the lamps, already burning poorly in the subterranean atmosphere, to take on a blue tint. The ground was studded with mounts that it was necessary to climb over or go around continually.

In other places, they had to pass between two walls that were inclined toward one another, and seemed to be supporting one another in perilous equilibrium. From time to time stones were detached; entire blocks fell, torn from matrices worn away by the centuries, obedient to a simple displacement of air or the vibrations provoked by the footsteps of the three companions, who had to employ all their agility to avoid those dangerous falls, which might have been mortal.

After an hour of walking in those terrible conditions they had scarcely covered two hundred meters, following the meanders of the tortuous path they had taken. They were still going upwards, to be sure, but there was no other indication that they were really going in the right direction. The narrow street appeared to continue for a long way yet, so far as they could judge by the sonority of their voices, which seemed to die away in unknown depths, and did not sent back any echoes.

The doctor offered the advice that they should get some rest, and fortify themselves at the same time by eating a meal, no matter how frugal. The three men installed themselves in a house whose open door had remained intact. They were harassed by fatigue, covered in sweat, and scarcely had the heart to devote themselves to archeological observations. Nevertheless, they were amazed by the spectacle offered to them by the house they had entered. It had resisted the cataclysm that had destroyed the city, and everything in it remained in a state of near-perfect preservation.

The dwelling had once sheltered a goldsmith. The room in with the mariners found themselves had served as his shop and his workshop. The house having sunk all of a piece, along with the ground on which it stood, without collapsing or its walls splitting, the organization of the accommodation had scarcely been disturbed. To the left, the workman's oven could still be seen, a brick mass garnished with a convex terra cotta mantle, outlining a kind of primitive furnace. Alongside it were placed the iron pipes that Egyptian goldsmiths had used in that remote era to obtain, simply by blowing through the pipes, the fusion of metals and enamels. In truth, those pipes had become masses of rust, and fell apart as soon as they were touched, but the general lines of their elongated form could still be clearly discerned, with a bulge near the tip, which terminated in a narrow outlet.

In a corner, on a low base, there was a lathe, still carrying the silver stalk on which the artist had been working at the moment of the earthquake. Alongside, on the scarcely worm-eaten wood of the support was the maple-wood bow that the turner maneuvered with his left hand in order to imprint the piece with its circular movement. Only the string had disappeared, leaving around the shaft the trace of the groove hollowed out by knot that had attached it.

In the middle of the room stood a low table supported by slightly-inclined legs, joined together by diagonal crossbars. Two jars were set on the table, and next to them were five silver cups. On the floor, a third jar with a pointed base rested on a wooden saddle; it was doubtless a jar of precious wine, and the unfortunate goldsmith must have been surprised by death among with his guests in the middle of a feast. Scattered around there were seats affecting the form of deck-chairs and two large wooden armchairs, in which incrustations of ivory or horn could still be seen, one of them tipped over. At the back there was a small iron cupboard, rusted and holed like an old wreck, and on the ground, ten small gold ingots: the jeweler's treasure, which he had tried to save in the panic of the flight, and part of which he had dropped.

Finally, on a sort of broad cyma made of brick that went all around the room, there was the artist's display, throwing off gleams of scarcely-tarnished gold under the light of the unfortunate explorers' lamps.

Such is the curious power of gold that the three men, disinterested in their everyday existence, incapable of an avaricious thought, presently occupied in disputing their lives with destiny, harassed and hungry, stopped before those riches and lingered, in spite of the frightful perils of the moment, passing them from hand to hand.

There were gold trays, sculpted with elegant floral designs surrounded by graceful hieroglyphs; cups reposing on the heads of bridled horses surmounted by pyramidal lids, bearing on each face the head of a goat with curved horns; fantastic spoons whose handles represented a dog with a fish in its mouth, the body of which, hollowed out, served as the hull of the utensil; vases of large dimension, recalling in their graceful design the pure forms of Greek amphorae, surrounded by garlands of lotus-flowers, with handles shaped like leaping gazelles. Then there was a marvelous collection of small objects: signet rings bearing the master's hieroglyph engraved on their stone, which took the place of a signature in legal formalities—which obliged every Egyptian to have his seal—and bracelets in lapis lazuli, cornelian and green feldspar, mounted on gold trellises and bearing the cartouches of those for whom they were destined on plaques. There were other bracelets recalling the facture of cloisonné enamels, covered in figures raised in relief in gold, the field being filled in by a blue paste the color of turquoise, or plaques of naturally colored stone. Finally, there were clasps representing scarabs with wings deployed, iridescent with enamel, or coupled hawks' heads; necklaces composed of strange flowers, torsades simulating ropes; and the sculpted hilts of daggers, ornamented with cornelian triangles and garnished by way of a pommel with four women's faces in embossed gold.

No matter how preoccupied they were, the unexpected visitors of that collection, three thousand years old, could not help admiring the excellence and ingenuity of that antique art, which had obtained such effects with such primitive means of execution.

"What a treasure for our museums," said the doctor, "If we were able to take these marvels back to the land of the living."

"Yes, Doctor," Georges replied, "but we can't. Let's take these rings and bracelets, which don't weight very much and won't slow us down, but leave the rest here."

"Yes, of course," said Quosé, "you're right. Let's leave the rest—although it's a great pity!" At the same time he turned in his hands one of the slender gold ingots, as broad as a small gun-barrel, which he had picked up near the artist's strong-box. "They're not very heavy, though, Commandant, these little pieces of gold—and *sapristi!* It would be a nice addition to my pension, especially if I take it as matelot second class, which will certainly hang me by the ears...always assuming that I ever return from the rank of mole to that of matelot, which isn't certain."

"That's true," said Georges. "Put those ingots in your pocket, my friend. You aren't rich, and that's not what will prevent us from saving ourselves."

"As for the rest," Halgouët said, "nothing prevents us from coming back to find it once we've seen daylight again."

"It's necessary not to count on that, my friend," replied Sergeant. "There's every chance that this house, which, by some phenomenon I can't yet explain has resisted the invasion of the waters for thirty centuries, like the rest of this fantastic city, will be inundated very soon. And I confess that I'm clawed by the dread of seeing that reckoning arrive at any moment. Given the nature of the *Sirius'* cargo, the action of sea-water might provoke massive releases of gas, under the pressure of which the ship will inevitably be displaced. If it quits the place where it's wedged even by ten centimeters, the water will invade this place in a matter of seconds. That's why I think we should only sit down for a moment—just long enough to rest and eat a little biscuit, and then resume our journey."

That observation recalled his companions to an awareness of the situation. They sat down on the ancient seats around the table laden with the amphorae of the Egyptian goldsmith's last feast; they opened the sack and shared a few broken biscuits, soaked in a small ration of water.

After a mere quarter of an hour, the troop resumed its difficult march.

Suddenly, the upward slope became much steeper. At the same time, the aspect of the alleyway changed. To the left there was no longer stone heaped up by human hands but veritable natural rock; to the right there was an enormous sheer wall, with no trace of any window or door, but constructed. A sensation of heat overtook the three mariners. Sweat inundated them; the atmosphere became much heavier; they seemed to be in a steam-bath. The doctor placed his hand on the wall of rock; it was so hot that he withdrew it immediately. At the same time, a sulfurous odor spread through the air.

"Well, this is something else," said the doctor.

"What?"

"It's not enough to have to contend with earth and water; now we have to deal with fire."

"Fire?"

"Yes. Have you noticed, Commandant, that the islet of Syrtos, close to which you must have passed without

154

stopping for as long as today, if often crowned with a light plume of smoke?"

"That's possible."

"It's certain. Well, my friend, at the moment we're going along the chimney of the volcano."

"From which you conclude?"

"To tell the truth, not much, for the moment. But that furnishes me with the solution to one of the problems that intrigued me—of explaining why we have air. The chimney at the bottom of which we find ourselves obviously communicates in places with the dead city. The latter, on the other hand, certainly has a channel to the open air, and the heat of the terrestrial fire determines a draught of air."

"Good," said Halgouët. "Very good—I'm very happy to have the explanation—but what do we need to do to find the channel to the open air?"

"It's necessary to continue, of course, and go as quickly as possible."

"That's what I thought," replied the Breton, a trifle sarcastically, wondering why a man of good sense like the doctor could occupying himself with searching for the solution to problems in such a situation. He forgot, with that astonishing logic peculiar to human nature, that he had been occupied himself with it for an hour before filing his pockets with gold ingots.

The aspect of the route changed at every step. The right-hand wall still extended its uniform façade, scarcely cracked in places. It was probably the enclosing wall of a temple. But the left-had wall was modified as they progressed. It had been broken, convulsed and sculpted by the cataclysm. Sometimes it opened a space six meters wide, sometimes it came so close to the wall that the mariners had to pass by in single file. In some places it allowed a glimpse of white, crystalline, sparkling veins of mica, in others broad green steaks of copper ore. It soon became entirely black, but a shiny black, reflecting the light in a thousand facets, like so many somber and strangely powerful mirrors.

"Look!" said the doctor. "Coal!"

"What! Coal in volcanic terrain! That's improbable."

"Why? Some small lake, which, in prehistoric times, has accomplished its work of transformation on submerged vegetable matter. And ultimately, there's no room for argument: just look!"

Georges de Malher drew closer, raising the bronze Egyptian lamp taken from the archers' guard-room to the level of his face. As he did so the flame flickered and turn blue.

"Put it out! Put them out!" exclaimed the doctor, setting the example. "And lie down!"

Georges and Halgouët obeyed instinctively. At the same moment a terrible explosion resounded, the earth trembled, a further revolution took place in the tortured ground, enormous blocks fell from the vault, and the three unfortunates remained lying on the ground, stunned by the shock, their hair singed, half-asphyxiated. They had fallen upon a pocket of firedamp.

Fortunately, the explosion had the effect drawing in air from the mysterious source that alimented the atmosphere of the dead city. Under that benevolent influence, the mariners recovered consciousness. They swallowed a gulp of eau-de-vie, of which the doctor had fortunately packed a bottle. Then they resumed walking, groping their way, and some distance further on, when they were sure that the air had been renewed, they struck the flint of a lighter and relit their lamps.

They observed then that the route had been completely blocked by the collapse of one of the walls under the influence of the firedamp explosion. Facing them was a granite wall; to the right, a path opened going along the wall of the temple—and that path sloped downwards.

V
The Granite Wall

They conferred momentarily. The situation was critical. If they took the only route left open to them, they would lose the ground they had gained—and yet, they had no alternative. Perhaps, a short distance away, they would discover some crossroads offering another rising path. Nevertheless, before entering the narrow corridor, they made sure that the route they were leaving behind was conclusively cut off.

They went back five hundred meters, as far as the collapse provoked by the firedamp explosion. It was necessary to yield to the evidence. An enormous mass of rock, which only the repose of time had maintained in a state of unstable equilibrium, had separated from the bank at a place where the path narrowed and had sealed it hermetically all the way to the vault. The stone that it would have been necessary to pierce to retrace their steps was at least ten meters thick. There was nothing at all to be attempted in that direction.

Even so, the doctor insisted on examining the nature of the enormous obstacle. Furthermore, he seemed to experience a kind of pleasure in ascertaining that the passage was solidly blocked. The accumulation of rocks presented a slope, which the irregularity of the surface permitted him to climb. He set down the bags he was carrying and tackled the ascent, with the lantern saved from the *Sirius* in his hand.

His companions did not understand that obstinacy, and reminded him that moments were precious. They were stamping impatiently, and a sentiment of bitterness was evident in their words. Halgouët was a simple, disciplined individual who certainly had a blind confidence in his two superiors; Georges' character was just and benevolent, but nevertheless, so deadly is the action of persistent misfortune, so hurtful the repercussion of continual disappointments, that the men were beginning to get irritated with one another, and they needed all their strength of mind to combat that intimate fermentation. It was in an imperious, almost harsh voice that Georges shouted: "Come back, Sergeant! No absurd obstinacy!"

"Listen to the Commandant," said Halgouët, supportively.

"Patience! Patience!" replied the doctor, suspended ten meters above the ground.

And from below, they watched the little light describing capricious curves while its invisible carrier continued his mysterious investigations.

The wait lasted ten minutes. Halgouët and Georges had sat down. The Commandant was tormenting the ground furiously with the end of one of the iron bars he was carrying. As for Quosé, unable to remain inactive and to seek a deflection of his anger in manual labor, he was busing weaving, with the thread taken from his shirt, a supplementary wick for the lamps.

Finally, the doctor came back down.

"You're impatient, my friends," he said, "but you won't hold it against me when I tell you the result of my research. I've acquired the certainty that a second collapse has occurred on the other side of the blockage."

"And what do you see that's so fortunate about that?" asked Georges.

"I simply see, my dear friend, the elements of a relative security. Here's why: all along the route that we've traveled, I've observed that the corridor in which we were formed a kind of tunnel. Almost always, on the right hand side, we were traveling alongside enormous walls composed of gigantic blocks of stone, piled up like the indestructible pelagic constructions of Mycenae. On the left hand side, there were houses, but they were back up against the rock of the hill that sheltered them; I noticed that in the goldsmith's house, where the back wall was formed by the rock itself. Now that the tunnel is sealed—and solidly, I beg you to believe—the water that will enter via the orifice that the *Sirius* is blocking can't reach us, at least not abruptly. To tell the truth, I don't believe that the dyke thus opposed to the sea can resist indefinitely; I'm equally certain that the water will fray a path through the walls, solid as they may be—but the inundation will only proceed henceforth in the form of a more or less rapid infiltration, and perhaps we'll have time to reach the source of fresh air."

"May God hear you!"

"He'll hear us."

"In the meantime," groaned Halgouët, "the only route open to us goes downwards."

"Perhaps it will rise again," the doctor replied, philosophically. "God knows what he's doing, my dear friend. One often complains of an evil that enables you to avoid something worse. If we weren't here, perhaps, at this very moment, we'd be victims of cholera in Beyrouth."

"We're not much better off."

"Perhaps so, but we're still alive. Come on, comrades—no discouragement, and let's go!"

The little troop resumed marching, and went into the descending corridor. The route was relatively easy, bordered on each side by resistant walls. While they walked, the doctor tried to build up his companions' morale.

"By the way," he said, "I've finally discovered why the dead city wasn't inundated. By climbing the blocks, I reached the vault, and recognized its nature: it's simply lava. I can explain what happened now; at the moment of the eruption the lava spread over the city, whose dimensions can't have been very considerable. In places, it arrived hot and still liquid, and flowed through the intervals of the streets. Elsewhere, it streamed in dense cascades, and then cooled again, forming buttresses between one row of houses and another, and serving, so to speak, as the framework of a vault constituted by the flow of igneous materials. Ash then covered and cemented that entire stony carapace. As we've had the proof by examining the gash opened in that armor along the flank of the Sirius, the ash had a texture akin to clay, and, once steeped in water, created a kind of envelope that blocked up the slightest fissure. Thus, once the ground sank downwards and the entire city was buried under water in its shroud of lava, the interior of the immense sepulcher was respected by the sea."

"That's plausible, in fact," Georges replied, "and I can't see any other explanation.

After that dialogue, they walked in silence. Halgouët had taken the lantern, whose light was the most powerful, and was marching ahead of his companions. Suddenly, he stopped, and the two officers saw him retrace his steps.

"There's no point going any further," he said.

"Why not?"

"The route is completely blocked. One might think that the vault comes all the way down to the ground. Take a look."

He raised his lantern. Indeed the ceiling came gradually lower, and met the ground twenty meters further on.

"That's unusual!" said the doctor. "We must have happened on one of the lava-flows that penetrated to the utmost depths of the streets."

"This time," said Georges, "I believe we're doomed."

Sergeant said nothing.

But Halgouët said: "Perhaps not entirely. At any rate, there's still one thing we can try."

"What? We can't get through this way, nor go back—and as for piercing the cyclopean wall we left behind us..."

"I've got it," said the doctor. "Halgouët wants to try a mine."

"No," Quosé replied. "For one thing, I don't think we have enough explosive to blast through a wall like this. For another, I think that the results of a further explosion are bound to get us crushed."

"That's true. So..."

"So, we have the resource of going under the wall."

Georges and the doctor looked at one another, wondering whether Quosé was in his right mind.

"I'm not mad," said the matelot, "only you scientists don't know everything. Me, I've only learned dribs and drabs of various things, but I've remembered everything. As I told you a while ago, the captain who taught me gave me a fair amount of information about the Egyptians, and I remember it as if it were yesterday. What you don't suspect is that these walls, so thick, so forbidding and so solid, have no foundations. The architects of that era simply placed the bottom layer on level ground. Even if the wall we have to get through is three or four meters thick, we simply have to dig a tunnel of that length in the earth. The idea occurred to me some time ago and I carefully inspected the nature of the soil at the top of the alleyway we've been following. I've seen that it simply consists of compact soil—hard, no doubt, but easy enough to shift with the iron bars we have. If prisoners, as I once read in *Latude, ou trente-cinq ans de captivité*,[8] have been able to dig through walls like those of the Bastille with a spoon-handle, I'll be damned if the three of us, with solid levers, can't dig a mole-hole four meters long and a meter in diameter through friable soil, quite rapidly."

"You're right, Halgouët," said the Commandant. "And perhaps it's you who are going to save us all."

"Each in his turn, Commandant," the Breton replied. "Only I don't know if you've noticed, but time's passing."

"In fact, what time of day is it?"

They had naturally brought their watches. The doctor's and Georges had stopped at the moment of the fire-damp explosion. Only Quosé's old onion, more primi-

---

[8] Jean-Henri Latude (1725-1805) recklessly tried to work a confidence trick on the Marquise de Pompadour, and was sent to the Bastille in 1749. After being transferred to Vincennes he escaped, but was recaptured and then began a long series of escape-attempts, which only achieved temporary success until he was finally released in 1784. In collaboration with Jean de Beaupoil he wrote an account of his imprisonment, *Despotisme dévoilé, ou Mémoires de Henri Masers de La Tude, détenu pendant trente-cinq ans dans les diverses prisons d'éta*t, which was published without the requisite royal stamp of approval in 1787 and became an underground best-seller in the run-up to the 1789 Revolution.

tive and more robust, had kept going. It said one o'clock. It was, therefore, one o'clock in the morning.

The decided to take some more nourishment—just the strictly necessary ration of biscuit and water—and then to rest, but only after having returned to the point where they would commence work. It was decided that, as usual, they each would take turns to keep watch, in order to warn his companions if there was a threat of collapse or some other danger.

The doctor asked to take the first watch. His companions, exhausted by fatigue, went to sleep as soon as they lay down. As for him, in accordance with his custom, he marched back and forth, only keeping the smallest lamp alight and devoting himself to calculations. After an hour, he was to be seen, like Archimedes at the siege of Syracuse, lying full length on the ground, with his sad light beside him, tracing figures and triangles in the soil, for want of paper, with a pebble, for want of a pencil.

When they woke up, he announced to his friends that he had established their approximate location.

"I've adopted the most favorably hypothesis," he told them. "The *Sirius*, as we know from the hydrography of the region, must have sunk to a bed between twenty and thirty brasses deep. Even if it was thirty brasses, given the slope that we followed and the distance we covered, we ought to be twelve or fifteen meters at the most below sea level. If we can only find a slope and free passage on the other side of this wall, we'll soon reach the level of the islet's emergence. There, we'll be able to employ the explosive to break through the vault."

They set to work. After scarcely twenty minutes, the lever under moderate effort, penetrated beneath the bottom of the wall. Halgouët was not mistaken; the construction had no foundations. The soil was harder than he had thought, though. By the end of the first day, the whole, dug obliquely, a meter in diameter, was only twenty-four centimeters long. Assuming that the wall was four meters thick, it would require five days to complete the task.

They made an inventory of the food and water. By rationing it in the most severe fashion, at six hundred grams of biscuit and a liter of water per twenty-four hours, there was scarcely sufficient, given the labor they had to undertake, to last the mariners a week.

The work did not stop, night or day; there was, in any case, no difference between night and day so far as the unfortunates buried underground were concerned, stubbornly defending their existence. Without the watches, with which Georges carefully kept track of the hours elapsed, marking each twenty-four hours with a thread knotted in a buttonhole, they would rapidly have most any notion of time. Ten days had passed since they had disappeared from the surface of the earth, and it seemed to them that that interval was a single frightfully long day, punctuated by periods of poor sleep.

They had inverted the proportion of the watches—which is to say that two of the companions were always awake while the third slept. It required, in fact, the combined efforts of two men to keep the work going. The first, lying in the hole, detached the earth with his lever; the second carried the debris out in a jacket that he held by the four corners.

After five days, they had gained the anticipated four meters, but the levers, entered as probes into the "sky" of the mine-shaft, still encountered a stone vault. Was the wall, then, thicker than they had thought?

On the evening of the sixth day, by means of a superhuman effort, they had conquered another meter. Halgouët, who as in the lead, tested the roof with his lever. He still felt anyone. Then, in a fit of anger, he delivered a violent blow to that rocky surface that seemed never-ending. The stone shattered like a thin crust; they were under a pavement.

With a thrust of his shoulder, the Breton lifted the paving-stone and emerged from the opening. His companions followed him; they were two meters from the wall. Deceived by the pavement, they had labored for two days for nothing!

The mariners had penetrated into an immense temple. Close by stood a gigantic statue in pink granite, representing a seated god, his hands rigidly extended on his knees. The companions did not spend much time looking at it. Facing them was a doorway. They went to it swiftly, and on the other side found a corridor, which did n not rise steeply, but which did slope upwards.

The doctor took the lead, while his friends loaded the tools and provisions—much diminished, alas! only sufficient for two days—on to their shoulders. Suddenly, he stumbled, and dropped his lamp.

As he bent down to pick it up, his gaze looked ahead, and he uttered a cry of amazement. The obscurity revealed a strange spectacle to him, which the lamplight had previously hidden. Twenty paces away there was a door, and in the frame neatly outlined by that door he saw...light!

VI
Pilgrimage

After the judgment of the court martial had acquitted Sir Owen, there was a change of opinion in his favor, and everyone saw him for what he really was: an unfortunate man worthy of universal esteem. The dispositions of the French colony were entirely modified. On the very evening of the trial, on the initiative of the French school in Athens, a gathering of our compatriots took place, and in that assembly the double resolution was taken to open a subscription to raise a monument to the victims of the *Sirius* on Syrtos, and to send a delegation to Sir Owen to make him party to that intention and simultaneously to express the sympathies of the French resident in Greece.

The following day, the delegation went to the hotel where Sir Owen was staying. It comprised three notables of the colony, a member of the French school and the director of that scholarly institution—the same one who had obtained, thanks to his considerable notoriety and his universally esteemed character, the right to carry out the successful excavations at Delphi that had attracted the attention of so many archeologists.

The meeting was moving in its cordiality. Sir Owen thanked our compatriots warmly, and replied to them that after the mental ordeals he had endured, no consolation could be more welcome than the step that had been taken in his regard.

"As regards the monument to be erected to the memory of the victims," he added, "permit me to take the sole responsibility for that. I have every right, since it's me who was the involuntary cause of the misfortune we deplore, and also because, as you know, George de Malher is my relative. I've already take steps to realize the project. The monument will be simple and severe, as is appropriate to honor soldiers who have died on the marine field of honor, the sea, while carrying out their duty. It will consist of a column on which a bronze plaque, tracing in its inscription an account of the disaster, will also express the dolorous regrets of the affection of the French fatherland and the loyalty of England. I beg you, Messieurs, to leave me the supreme satisfaction of that final duty. I believe, in any case, that you can follow nevertheless the pious inspiration that has guided you, and nothing prevents you, if you will permit me to give you the advice, from erecting the monument that you have projected within the grounds of the admirable French school, which is so highly appreciated by all the literate people of the world. The victims will thus receive a double tribute. Mine, on the Greek islet, testifying to the death of those brave men, will be the public reparation of my country. Yours, on the corner of French soil that the school represents, will be the testimony of your intimate grief. I hope that you will not oppose matters passing thus?"

"The sentiments that you express, Monsieur," the head of the delegation replied, "are too noble not to find an echo in our hearts. With regard to ourselves, we incline before your reasons; we shall render an account of your intentions to those who sent us, and we believe that we can already reply on their behalf that that things will proceed in accordance with your desires."

Numerous individual visits succeeded the collective step by the French colony, but Sir Owen, who was occupied with other matters, entrusted the care of receiving them to one of his friends, as well as the task of replying to the local newspaper reporters and representatives of the foreign press who flocked to his door wanting to interview him.

The latter would not admit defeat, however. They waited for him at street-corners, surprised him in restaurants, watched for him in the offices of the bank from which he drew his funds. He found them on the stairs of the French consulate, at the door of the English legation and in the shop of the stonemason from which he had commissioned the monument. He saw them emerging from the workshop of the founder who was to fabricate the bronze plaque, from the harbor of Piraeus, and even from the bath-house. Finally, while handing in a dispatch at the counter of the telegraph office, he was astounded to hear the employee say to him, with his most gracious expression: "In addition to being a functionary, sir, I'm a reporter for *The Athens Messenger*, and you won't hold it against me if I seize the unexpected opportunity offered to me to ask you for your impressions of the trial, the outcome of which we all applaud..."

As one can imagine, confronted by that obsession, the captain of the *Investigator* was in even greater haste to escape its manifestations, sympathetic as they were, and return to Syrtos in order to conclude the dolorous mission that he had given himself. So, in the evening of the day after the trial, he returned to Piraeus after having completed, with his usual activity, all that he had to do in Athens. He planned to make the final arrangements with the Port Authority the following morning, in order that, as soon as the refloated *Sirius* arrived, the ship could be put in dry dock and repaired. He had already given orders that the steamer that had brought him back should be ready to put to sea.

Indeed, the following morning, at eleven o'clock, he had resolved all the difficulties and was preparing to go back to the hotel for a rapid lunch when someone came to tell him that his niece had arrived and was waiting for him.

The poor young woman had recovered from her illness and immediately wanted to resume her voyage. We shall not describe the meeting of Sir Owen with his niece; as can be imagined, it was infinitely dolorous. For Sir Owen it was the last stage of the trail of tears that he had been following for three weeks. It was even more poignant than the others.

From the very first words, Sir Owen observed that Madame de Malher was still prey to the obsession that her husband was not dead, and he had to undertake the sad task of reasoning with her unhappiness in such a way as to make her understand that her misfortune was irreparable. However, he ran into a deep-rooted conviction all the more unshakable because, not resting on any deduction, drawing its force from some mysterious instinct, she would not allow it to be eroded either by arguments or by facts.

To everything that her devoted relative said to her, Madame de Malher replied, raising her eyes to the heavens, softly but with a strange firmness: "What do you expect, Uncle! It's a matter of faith, and faith doesn't debate."

It was so much a matter of faith that the young woman, during her illness, had made a vow: that she would go, before embarking, to the last Catholic sanctuary that she found on her route before leaving, to ask God to return her husband to her. And she had added an aggravation to that vow which offered testimony to her faith and her Christian humility.

There was no Catholic church in Piraeus. The only temple that could receive her fervent prayer was a small private chapel attached to the château of M. A***, a French engineer resident in the country who, having made a considerable fortune in the construction of Hellenic lighthouses, had built a beautiful country house on the cliff three kilometers from Piraeus. A messenger went to ask him, on behalf of Madame de Malher, for permission to come during the day to pray in that oratory, and authorization was granted by our compatriot with the most courteous and respectful urgency.

At three o'clock, the young woman left the hotel where she had taken a room. With her natural elegance, she was wearing a simple black costume, but not mourning-dress—because, believing that her husband was not dead, she refused to dress as a widow. In spite of her youth and the flexibility of her gait, she seemed to have difficulty walking, but she refused the support of Sir Owen's arm as he accompanied her.

The passers-by stopped and looked at the woman, young and beautiful, with a calm and inspired expression, her eyes lowered as if in prayer, who appeared to be having so much difficulty following her course. They divined something strange in the foreigner's apparent stroll, and when, almost at every step, she stumbled on the pebbles of the path and her foot appeared at the edge of her dress, they saw with an indescribable astonishment that the lady, so graceful in her somber clothing, was wounding feet that were entirely naked on the rude asperities of the road.

Sir Owen was penetrated by a reluctant but emotional admiration for that obstinate confidence, in which he could not see anything but a touching manifestation of folly. At times, so contagious is faith, he began to

171

wonder himself whether, by some inexplicable miracle, the missing men might still be alive. He was obliged, to his great astonishment, to appeal to his reason to respond to the doubt that rose within him.

While shrugging his shoulders before that absurd and vague hope, which he could not even define, and which nevertheless summoned the denial of reasoning, he associated himself with his relative's pious step. He experienced a need to impose upon himself, beside that Christian woman who was wounding her bare feet on thorns, a suffering akin to her own, and it was with his hat in his hand, and the hot autumn sunlight falling upon his gray head, that he walked along the high cliff, where both of them could look out over the blue sea, in which the young woman stubbornly refused to see a tomb.

That same evening, Madame de Malher and Sir Owen left for Syrtos, where they arrived at first light.

The personnel left in place by the captain of the *Investigator* had used the time profitably. The *Sirius* was entirely afloat, and was almost able to sustain herself without the aid of the floats that surrounded her like an immense lifebelt. Poulpiquet and the divers had been working hard. The enormous rip made in the hull of the *Sirius* by the prow of the *Investigator* had been provisionally patched in such a way as to ensure sufficient impermeability.

The work had not been easy, given that the hull was made of iron, and they did not have the equipment necessary to apply a metallic lining to the wound, into which nails could not be driven as into a wooden hull, but the initiative of the French engineer and Sir Owen's first mate had made up for the insufficiency of means.

An internal patch had been place over the rip composed of six layers of strong sailcloth, seen together with greased thread. The same operation had been carried out externally. Between the two patches a thick layer of greased oakum had been pressed, and then the two had been stitched together like a mattress. After that, a trellis of thick wooden laths had been arranged over the ensemble, inside and out, in such a way that the internal framework was linked to the external one by strong screws driven through the canvas and the oakum, compressing them between the two structures. The square hole pierced by the mariners imprisoned in the hold had been blocked in the same fashion.

The pumps had then gone to work and the unfortunate vessel, emptied of the water that had invaded her, in which everything had been turned upside down, almost all the partitions staved in, the engines rusted and the woodwork of the cabins disjointed, but on the whole, not badly damaged by the catastrophe, would be able, after wholesale repairs, to be returned to France.

Satisfied with that, Sir Owen gave generous gratifications to all those who had taken part on the reflotation, thanked the French engineer effusively, and decided that the two steamers would tow the *Sirius* back to the Greek coast the following day.

One of the two would bring back the material and the personnel necessary for the erection of the monument. In the meantime, the location would be chosen and the foundations dug.

Sir Owen considered that he ought to take the advice of Madame de Mahler with regard to the site of the column. Given her present state of mind, however, he anticipated that she would refuse to intervene. Was not the monument almost a tomb, and was not Madame de

Malher refusing to believe that her husband was dead? In broaching the subject with her, he was simply obeying what he considered to be a rigorous duty.

To his great surprise, Madame de Malher replied: "Thank you. If you wish, we'll land on Syrtos tomorrow, and we'll choose the location together."

VII

A Chink of Sky

It is difficult to form an idea of the surprise—one might almost say the terror—that was provoked in the guests of the dead city by the sight of that door, in the frame of which light was visible. The fact was so improbable, so incredible, that no hypothesis came immediately to mind that might explain it, and they experienced a sentiment of surprise that was tinged with fear.

Before going any further, they extinguished the other lamps, which when lit, no longer allowed the phenomenon to be seen. There was no mistake about it; they could not believe that it was a sensory error; they could distinctly see a light—faint, to be sure, similar to that cast in a mortuary chamber by the dying lamp of a victim destined for burial, but nevertheless perfectly perceptible. Was the chamber thus illuminated receiving an indirect reflection of exterior daylight? That was the only explanation admissible.

They struck the flint of a lighter, relit the lamps, and with their hearts beating poignantly, they headed for the opening.

The door gave access to an exceedingly large room, and at first glance it was easy to observe that it did not offer any issue through which a ray of daylight might be introduced. The room was cluttered with an accumulation of objects of singular shape, the nature of which it was difficult to determine at first glance. On looking more attentively, the mariners recognized to their left huge piles of wood, disposed in regular structures by

175

layers of planks placed at right angles to one another. To the right, there were crates of some sort, affecting rounded and eccentric forms, similarly piled up methodically. Along the walls, similar crates stood, piled up against the wall, giving the vague impression of human forms larger than nature.

The three men realized that they were in the workshop of a carpenter who had specialized, three thousand years ago, in the manufacture of coffins and sarcophagi. The place was lugubrious, and, given the situation the mariners were in, the spectacle of those coffins, deprived of their anticipated guests by a cataclysm, was not calculated to revive their courage. Thus, they were in haste to quit the carpenter's abode, as soon as they had acquired the proof that the light they had glimpsed had not come from outside.

Nevertheless, they wanted an explanation of the strange phenomenon that had caused them a moment of surprise and had given them a momentary hope, so soon disappointed. They made the decision to extinguish the lamps again, and perceived then that the luminous effluvia were coming from a pile of wood attacked by damp resulting from some invisible infiltration, partly carbonized by that action and the action of time, the ridges of which presented phosphorescent streaks in numerous places. Quosé remembered having seen a similar phenomenon in his childhood on the trunks of trees that had spent a long sojourn in a pond, or wrecks cast up by the sea on the coast of his native Brittany.

As soon as the lamps were relit, the phosphorescence disappeared, and they resumed their route after one more disappointment.

The route continued to slope upwards, almost imperceptibly. The gradient was no more than a few millimeters per meter, and in certain curves the terrain of-fered nothing but a level surface. From time to time they had to clear the passage, encumbered by blocks of lava fallen from the vault or collapses of the lateral walls. It took a long time for the three men, fatigued by the strug-gle that they had sustained for such a long time, poorly fortified by insufficient and insubstantial nourishment, to clear a path. Thus, in the final hours of that day they on-ly gained a few hundred meters beyond the carpenter's workshop.

At nine o'clock in the evening they arrived at the end of the road; in that place, a new barrage awaited them: a wall formed by lava flows, a kind of grille with enormous, irregular bars almost welded together by a sheaf of tightly-clustered stalactites and warped by the effect intense volcanic heat that had almost brought them down to ground level. In the middle there was a gap, to narrow to allow a man to pass, but which it might be possible to widen if the stone as not too hard.

Georges proposed that they start the operation im-mediately, but Quosé and the doctor were absolutely worn out.

"Let's rest for a few hours, my poor friend," said Sergeant. "I can assure you that, in spite of all my ener-gy, I'm completely incapable of wielding an implement. Halgouët's like me, and, in spite of your courage, you couldn't furnish a sufficient effort."

"But remember that, even by diminishing our ration of water and biscuit by half, we only have enough food for forty-eight hours!"

"I know—but it's better, in spite of everything, to store up a little strength in our enfeebled bodies."

"So be it," said the Commandant. "Go to sleep. I'm not so tired, so I'll stay awake."

"I'll relieve you in two hours, Commandant," murmured Halgouët, who was lying on the ground with his head on a stone, already invaded by torpor.

As soon as the two friends were asleep, Georges picked up one of the iron levers. He took the little lamp made from an iron mug, placed it on the obstacle, and started attacking one of the stalactites bordering the central fissure. Once that obstacle was broken, the open space would be wide enough to let a man through, sideways on.

Just as he was about to strike the first blow with the lever he noticed, to his astonishment, that the tiny flame of his lamp was vacillating. He was far enough away not to be able to attribute the oscillation to the displacement of air provoked by him. To make sure of that, he remained completely still. The little lamp continued flickering.

Georges moved closer to the central opening. Without any possible doubt, he recognized that air was coming in through that opening—not the heavy and mephitic air that had been breathing thus far, but fresh and pure air, in which his mariner's senses found, delightedly, the vivifying perfume of briny emanations.

He filled his lungs with that air, which seemed to be a miraculous messenger of life. Then he woke his companions, numbed by their heavy slumber, forced them to get up, and led them to the orifice. He had no need to add any explanation to the action.

"Air!" they both cried. "Sea air!"

They picked up levers, and in less than an hour the combined efforts of the three men, multiplied tenfold, had reckoned with the obstacle.

They went through the issue, and found themselves in an immense grotto, a kind of air-hole, a giant bubble imprisoned, at the moment of the cataclysm, by a powerful discharge of gas, in the incandescent mass of the lava. Above their heads, the action of time had caused the igneous rock to rumble, and a large circular opening appeared at a height of fifty meters. Around the edges of the opening they could see the black silhouettes of tufts of tamarisk leaning over it under the influence of a wind that was agitating their stems and making itself felt even in the depths of her cavern, Great white clouds were passing overhead.

The three companions, mute, not daring to believe in the dream, watched the clouds going by, and when the long silver ribbon had unfurled, and the somber blue of the sky revealed, though the final gap, brilliant dots scintillating in the celestial vault, the doctor shouted: "The sky, my friends! The stars!"

"Yes, the stars," Georges replied. "And look, Doctor, Halgouët, do you recognize that constellation, that triangle of stars the summit of which is marked by the brightest star in the sky? That triangle is Canis Major, my friends, and the resplendent star at its summit is Sirius!"

The mariners could not tire of contemplating the sky, which appeared to them at the moment when, harassed by fatigue, weakened by privations and discouraged by attempts continually made and incessantly disappointed, they felt ready to succumb and abandon themselves. They held hands, and an ardent action of grace, devoid of formula or words, one of those sublime prayers that nothing can translate, which only the infinite gratitude of the soul can conceive, and which only God can understand, rose from their hearts toward that beautiful sky, the unexpected sight of which promised life, contact with beloved humans, a return to earth, an end to terrible ordeals.

The star that they contemplated with a kind of mild intoxication, other eyes—perhaps dear eyes—had seen and followed. Those clouds fringed with silver, which masked it from time to time, had passed over cities, over forests, over seas furrowed by ships, over rivers with populated banks. Perhaps they were going to the distant fatherland. Perhaps the droplets of water suspended in their fleecy swirls would fall as dew on the roofs of paternal dwellings, on the flowers of gardens that witnessed happy childhoods. For the exiles exhausted by the struggle and long suffering, that radiant chink of sky was almost the homeland.

"Yes, the homeland," said Halgouët. "The beloved country!"

"No," my friends," said Georges, "it's not yet the promised land, but I hope we'll be luckier than the patriarch, and that we'll reach it. Except that we have to help ourselves, if we want God to help us."

"That's true," replied Quosé and the doctor, recalled to reality by the walls. "We still have to reach the orifice of that cavern, and as it's situated in the middle of the vault, we still have some difficulties to overcome before getting there. But we've seen many others, haven't we?"

"Undoubtedly. So let's discuss what course to adopt right away."

"The first thing that springs to mind is to signal our presence here, to attract the attention of anyone who might be on the islet. But that's problematic—in fact, the islet is deserted. It's exceedingly rare for fishermen to land on it, and we don't know, in any case, whether the opening communicates with an accessible part of the surface."

"We could light a fire with the coffin-merchant's wood," said Quosé. "The column of smoke might attract attention."

"No, for that column of smoke would be confused from the sea with the fumaroles that still crown the crater, and wouldn't, in consequence, awaken any curiosity in those who saw it."

"I still have my provision of explosives," said Sergeant. "Perhaps a loud detonation would reveal our presence."

"It would first be necessary for someone to be on the islet. Even then, they'd certainly attribute it to some belated interior commotion of the volcanic ground."

"To reject our advice like that, Commandant," said the doctor, "you must have a idea of your own, and it must be good."

"I do, indeed, have an idea," Georges replied, "and I think it's good, because putting it into execution only depends on us. That idea is simply to make a ladder fifty meters high, and to use the coffin-maker's materials for that construction."

"But my dear friend, all that heaped-up wood is rotten. One might, strictly speaking, make a fire by utilizing the carbonized parts, but it seems to me to be impossible to make a ladder."

"You're right with regard to the mass of raw wood, but with regard to the coffins, I'm certain that Quosé, who, as we've seen knows a great deal about ancient Egypt, won't share your opinion."

"The Commandant's right, Doctor," replied Halgouët, proud to see Georges appealing to his knowledge. "You know that the dead play an important role among the Egyptians, and that no other people has pushed respect for the departed as far. A multitude of wooden sarcophagi have reached us absolutely intact, after having spent thousands of years in hypogea. The coatings with which they're daubed have not only preserved the wood from all deterioration, but have even kept the paintings and the hieroglyphics as fresh and bright as the day they were made. The people who invented the most advanced methods of embalming had very precise notions about the manner of preserving the wood that served for their sarcophagi as well as the bandages in which their mummies were wrapped from the putrefaction of centuries. I believe we'll be able to discover among the carpenter's coffins a sufficient number of preserved items for us to find the materials necessary to establish, if not a ladder, at least a parrot-mast, whose bars can be replaced by alternating notches. We don't need anything more."

The doctor yielded to these arguments, and the little troop, after one last glance at the sky, returned rapidly to the carpenter's workshop.

VIII
Life via Death

It was immediately decided only to stay long enough in the coffin-maker's store to gather the necessary materials, and that they would then come back to make the ladder in the place where it was to be used. Georges de Malher had made the remark, rightly that transporting a single piece of carpentry fifty meters long through the twists and turns of the route would pose the greatest difficulties. As for the construction of the ladder itself, even though they had no tools, the three companions did not doubt the possibility for a moment. Their mariners' ingenuity would substitute once again for the necessary instruments.

Their first concern, naturally, was to make an inventory of the resources that the funereal depot offered them. At the first inspection, they recognized that the piled-up wooden beam would, indeed, be no use to them. Only the exterior contours of the stacks retained the appearance of a regular arrangement of planks and joists. In the places that had not been carbonized, the texture of the completely-rotted wood offered no resistance and the fibers, reduced to pulp, gave way under the pressure of a finger. The ensemble was no longer anything but a soft mass of crumbling sheets, welded together. They fell back immediately on the coffins.

At first they experienced a further disappointment; those which were piled in stacks, filing the right hand half of the chamber, were scarcely any better conserved than the wood. On the other hand, fifty of the sarcophagi stood up against the walls were perfectly intact. That immunity was due to two causes. Firstly, the sarcophagi separated from the others had evidently been prepared with a view to imminent usage—which is to say that they were completely finished, and clad in a preservative coating. Secondly, a certain number of them, prepared with particular care, must have been destined for rich clients, and in order to make them worthy of their guests, the workman had exhausted all the procedures of his art.

The latter were formed as sheaths, approximately reproducing the contours of the bodies they were to contain. The walls were seven or eight centimeters thick, made of a kind of sycamore wood, which, thanks to the preparation, had become even harder under the action of time. Not a single nail entered into their fabrication; all the assemblies had been made either with pegs or long acacia thorns. All around them ran inscriptions and hieroglyphics carefully traced in black on the white coating. Inside, other inscriptions contained a prayer for the deceased and passages from *The Book of the Dead*, a kind gospel of Egyptian funerary liturgy.

Alongside those sarcophagi were their lids, vaguely designing a recumbent human figure, with a square wig framing the face with long almond-shaped eyes enameled in white whose intensely black pupils seemed to be gazing into infinity. The hands, painted in vermilion, were joined, holding an ansate cross—a kind of cross whose short upper branch was in the form of a loop, and which, in the Egyptian religion, was the symbol of life.

The carpenter had not only concerned himself with the coffins; alongside those was an infinity of objects—all the accessories of death, which, among the Egyptians, took on an extremely complex form: tiny seats and tables, household utensils of every sort, statuettes representing gods and goddesses, chests to contain the clothing of the deceased. The Egyptian dead, in fact, had to take with them, as much as possible, a complete set of movable property, and even the poorest families strove to conform to custom by enclosing with the mummies of their relatives simulacra or cheap miniatures of the objects necessary to life.

Chairs and furniture of all shapes and sizes were falling into dust. Quosé and Georges searched through that host of strange things, however, in the hope of finding something that would help them in their task. The rectangular chests with convex lids or two panels like a roof of a house, had resisted best, but the metallic parts were entirely corroded by rust and the iron bands surrounding the coffers, which might have been useful, were as friable as poorly baked brick.

After a few minutes of investigation, the doctor, who had been carefully examining the sarcophagi and taking measurements, declared that there was more wood there than they needed to fabricate a beam with several pieces joined together, which could attain the required height. It remained now to find the necessary tools. All they had at their disposal presently were two iron bars and Quosé knife; that was very little.

"It's sufficient to break up the sarcophagi," said the doctor, "and by sharpening the end of one of the iron bars on the paving-stones we'll have an instrument sufficient trenchant to split the thick planks that we obtain lengthwise. But the difficulty that stops me is fitting the different components together. Our mast in fact, has to be a set of thin joists. In addition, there are the steps. We don't have any nails or cables. Strictly speaking, we could make pegs with Halgouët's knife, but in addition to the fact that we'd require a considerable quantity, which would take us a long time, we don't have anything akin to a drill, or the most primitive gimlet to pierce the holes destined to receive them."

"Listen, Doctor, let's not throw in the towel. Perhaps we'll find what we need in here. As there's no time to waste, let's make a start, with the Commander's aid, in sharpening the levers. In the meantime, I'll continue my search. Look, there's a kind of mill in this dark corner which the workman must once have used. It no longer has a handle or a frame, it's true, but we can pass one of our levers through the central hole, wedge the mill on that axle with a piece of wood and support the two ends on the two sides of a sarcophagus in which I'll hollow out two notches with my knife. It'll be necessary to turn the mill by hand, of course, which is, I admit, a trifle primitive as a method, but it will still be faster than wearing away the tip on the paving-stones."

The doctor and Georges immediately set to work. As for Quosé, he took the lantern from the *Sirius* and started rooting through the piles of materials, demolishing them, exposing all the objects that the stacks masked, scrutinizing the corners of the walls and testing the sonority of the ground with taps of his heel.

"What are you looking for, Halgouët?"

"Do you want to know, Commandant? I'm looking for something with which to make ropes."

"And you hope to find what you need to make ropes?"

"I'm almost sure of it. It's all a matter of finding the cupboard—and as the cupboard might be a cellar, a sort of silo, I'm trying to discover where it is."

While speaking, the Breton pulled toward him a funereal bed that must have been a veritable work of art. In the worm-eaten wood, one could still make out the figures of two elongated lions that formed the frame of the ceremonial couch, the tails of which curled round to interlace at the mummy's feet. But Quosé was scarcely disposed to admiration. He displaced the bed, which broke under his effort, and in the place where it had been a large projecting flagstone appeared, still presenting the holes of two iron rings.

Georges and Sergeant interrupted their work and helped him to raise the paving-stone, which was not very heavy. They laid bare a cavity into which one descended by a stairway of six steps. The floor was covered with a fine sand, and the walls of the cellar, into which the mariners immediately descended, were covered by a hard cement that rendered the place completely dry.

At the back, stone jars, which had contained the carpenter's provision of wine, were stacked on top of each other in a regular fashion. All trace of liquid had disappeared, naturally, and nothing remained at the bottom of the amphorae but the dark residue left by the slow evaporation of wine through the pores of terra cotta stoppers.

Other jars of larger dimension were buried up to the neck in the sand. One of them was open, and half-full of a substance that it was impossible to identify: a kind of coarse gray powder. The others were carefully sealed by stone lids hermetically closed with a thick layer of clay. They prized off one of the lids and, to the great astonishment of the three companions, they found that it was filled to the rim with wheat, the ears of which seemed to have been harvested the day before. The carpenter's winter reserve, thanks to the fashion in which it had been stored, and probably thanks to the nature of the soil in which the jars had been buried, had resisted the effects of time, and it was with a joyful surprise that the doctor realized that the three-thousand-year-old wheat could add a precious reinforcement to the meager ration of food they had left.

Finally, Quosé, who had continued his research, uttered a sudden cry of triumph.

"I've found it!" he exclaimed. "We're certain now of being able to make our ladder. Look!"

He pointed at a number of thin bales, each one as big as a paving-stone, which lay on the dry sand in the midst of a number of receptacles, in glass or terra cotta, of various shapes and sizes. The objects had once been set on shelves attached to the wall but the shelves had given way. Among the debris there were bottles and cups. It was in his cellar that the carpenter had kept his unguents and the substances necessary for embalming, and the bales at which Quosé was pointing were rolls of the linen bandages with which mummies were swathed. Those bandages had been shielded from the corruption of time by one of the balms that the Egyptians possessed, and maintained in a perfect state of conservation and solidity.

"Look," said the Breton, "we ought to have here perhaps two or three thousand meters of bandages. When I saw that the carpenter who is presently according us his involuntary hospitality had all the articles concerned with his estate, I immediately thought that he ought to possess a large stock of prepared bandages, and that's why I continued my search. By weaving together these long strips four at a time—of which I'll take charge, in my capacity as a matelot, who understands splicing better than anyone else, we'll obtain good cables, which will permit us to do without pegs and nails."

"It's a bizarre thing," the doctor added, philosophically, "to think that it's these accessories of death—

coffins and bandages—that are perhaps going to render life to us!"

After that discovery, they hastened to complete the preparations. They finished sharpening the levers, which, thanks to the mill, did not take long. Then they set about dismantling the sarcophagi.

After three hours, they had obtains a hundred pieced of wood, varying in section from six to eight centimeters. The operation had been relatively straightforward, the boards of the sarcophagi having been shaped following the grain of the wood.

It was Georges who had determined the number of planks to be fabricated. He had judged, in fact, that it would be very arduous and perhaps very dangerous to construct with all the pieces of wood they transported a unique mast as high as a four-story house, and he had decided, with the agreement of his companions, to replace it with a slightly pyramidal pylon with four faces, with edges constructed of beams connected to one another by cross-beams in the shape of St. Andrew's crosses. They would thus avoid the difficult task of setting up, without lifting-tackle and a derrick, a fifty-foot mast made of sections, whereas they could erect the pylon rapidly on the spot, attaching the pieces one after another.

Once the wood was assembled, they took the largest sarcophagus of all—an enormous coffin more than two meters long that had been made to serve as an envelope for two or three containers. They filed it with wood and the rest of the provisions, the jars of wheat and a quantity of carbonized planks with which to make a fire. By means of the first rope woven from the bandages they towed that sled all the way to the cavern, widening the opening in the barrage of stalactites to get it through. It required three trips to bring back all the materials required to get the work under way.

It would have been a strange spectacle to see, those three pale men dragging the coffin that contained all of their hopes through the somber streets of the dead city, by the faint light of their lamps, which designed small vague aureoles in the thick darkness.

Quosé's watch indicated five o'clock when they had finished. The three men, already harassed by the previous eight hours, who had just worked all night with an effort capable of fatiguing a healthy and robust individual, did not even think of lying down to sleep. They remained standing, their eyes fixed on the corner of the celestial vault where the stars were beginning to pale.

"What are you waiting for, Georges?" asked the doctor, smiling.

"The same thing you're waiting for, my friend," the Commandant replied, extending his hands to his two companions.

"Daylight, of course," said Halgouët. "The beautiful light of the sun."

In their impatient waiting there was a kind of meditation, something of the sentiment that the first human must have experienced when, after the frightful darkness that fell upon the first day, he saw, with infinite gratitude toward the Almighty, the return of the radiant light that he had thought lost forever.

Gradually, the stars paled further. The azure of the sky whitened; it passed from purple to soft pink; then it became clear blue: a transparent blue. At the same time, the light, the blessed light, fell into the depths of the grotto, illuminating the walls of rock, revealing verdant mosses, dwarf lichens, little ferns, almost vaporous maidenhair ferns: an entire humble vegetation, very poor and very modest, but which brought the unfortunate castaways the sentiment of life, which extracted them from terrible things and dead things, and gave them the notion with which their entire being vibrated, that at that moment they had ceased to be sad creatures lost in the abyss who, for so many mortal hours, had disputed their lives with all the united forces of nature and extinct civilization.

The first ray of sunlight the penetrated the depths of the cavern, cutting obliquely through the penumbra like an immense dart of translucent gold in which tiny particles of dust were scintillating, found the three men silent, lost in the same mute ecstasy. And when lassitude finally reclaimed its rights, when it was necessary to lie down on the mossy earth of the grotto and demand, like Antaeus, new strength from the mother of nature, it was by a spontaneous movement that all three went to lie down in the exact spot where that beneficent beam designed on the ground the resplendent circle of its vivifying light.

IX
Water!

When they awoke, a further surprise awaited them. The sky was cloudy. Rain was falling. The mouth of the grotto was evidently on a declivity of the volcanic cone, and a trickle of water was running into a cavern in miniature cascades. As can be imagined, that gift was extremely welcome.

Thanks to the carpenter's wheat, they were certain of not dying of hunger if the construction of the pylon required more time than they had anticipated, but they had not been sure of not dying of thirst; the water-skin brought from the Sirius only contained three liters of the water distilled by the doctor—bad water, besides, which almost provoked nausea by virtue of the odor it had acquired as a result of its long sojourn in the rubberized fabric.

They immediately unstitched one of the sacks and extended it beneath the waterfall, taking care to elevated its edges, and were able to collected a fairly considerable quantity of water, which they stored in the skins. At the same time, the mariners seized the opportunity to render vigor to their limbs by abundant ablutions. Under the beneficent shower, their skin became more supple and their pores recovered their elasticity.

They lit a fire, and used the metallic mugs to cook loaves of a sort, with flour made with the Egyptian carpenter's wheat. They ground the wheat between two stones, and confected cakes—which, to tell the truth, lacked flavor and were slightly offensive to the palate by reason of the absence of salt, but whose crunchy crust, obtained on the red-hot walls of the mug, and especially their warmth, were very agreeable to the three companions.

After having fabricated a certain number of those loaves, they attacked the construction of the pylon with a new ardor. While Georges and the doctor took the pieces of wood and arranged them in order of their dimensions, Quosé wove his four-ply cable, and it must be admitted that they went to work very quickly. That day, they raised the tower three meters above the ground, even though, by reason of the various preparations, the collection of the water and the confection of food supplies, they had only worked on it for half a day.

During the night, they did not organize watches. They all slept for about four hours, after which they went back to work. The project advanced rapidly. Nevertheless, it became increasingly difficult as the height increased, because of the necessity to taking up the pieces of wood. Georges worked alone at the summit. The doctor passed him the wood from below, which the doctor hoisted up by means of a cable, and joined to the construction by means of strong mariner's knots. Quosé continued to weave the cords.

By the evening of the second day they had edified a further four meters, which, added to the previous day's three, represented a total height of seven meters; they had done almost half of the work. They had regained not merely courage but entire confidence. A sentiment of tranquility for the future invaded the three men, who had been assailed thus far by such terrible anguish, and they experienced an invisible wellbeing, an unknown sensation of repose, in allowing themselves to be cradled by that return to normal life, characterized by healthy labor in the open air and broad daylight.

The consequence of that state of mind was that they went to bed earlier than usual that evening; sleep, as the relaxation of their nerves succeeded the unhealthy tension of great crises, resumed all of its empire, and it had been light for some time when Halgouët was the first to wake up, and shook his companions, who were still asleep, vigorously.

"I beg your pardon, Commandant," he said, joyfully, "for putting my hand on my officer, but it's for the good of the service. It's a matter of working, and although we've all slept well, I confess that I wouldn't be sorry to spend tomorrow night elsewhere than here, even if it's in the cabin of a fishing-boat noxious with the odor of fish."

The previous evening, Halgouët had entirely completed weaving his cable, which he had set down, properly rolled up, at the foot of the pylon. During the first part of the day he worked alongside Georges at the top of the scaffolding, while the doctor continued, as he had the day before, passing the wood up to them. They constructed another two meters.

At that moment, it seemed to the Commandant and Halgouët that the light tower vacillated slightly under their weight.

"It's evident," said Georges, "that our joists are a trifle weak. I think it would be prudent if one of us were to go down again. I think the edifice with resist the weight of one man, but not the weight of two."

"So be it," said Quosé. "Go down, Commandant."

"No, my friend," said Georges. "I think, without meaning to offend your self-esteem, that I can tie knots faster than you. You've rendered enough service for me simply to observe the fact, without any other concern than that of proceeding more rapidly."

"The fact is that you twist a hawser like a first-class able seaman. All right, I'll go down."

Having arrived at the bottom, Quosé said to the doctor: "Shall I help you, then?"

"To do what. I'm sufficient to the task on my own. You'd only get in my way, my worthy man."

"I'm just going to fold my arms, then?"

"Yes, while waiting for me to get tired. Then you can take my place."

"As you wish. Well, you know what? Instead of staying here doing nothing, I'm going to pay one last visit to the house of the excellent Egyptian carpenter."

"That's an odd whim—but after all, if you're determined..."

"My God, it's not that I'm determined, but perhaps you haven't noticed this..."

While speaking, he exhibited an exceedingly thin metal plate about fifteen centimeters by ten, which he had slipped into the pocket of his ragged jacket.

"Oh!" said the doctor. "But that's gold!"

"Yes, Doctor. I found it among the bottles and packets of bandages. Very rich Egyptian mummies were often armored with sheets of gold, and our coffin-merchant, who, as we've perceived, was a man of foresight and a businessman on a large scale, had to possess some. So I'm going to see if I can find some more."

"Ah, yes!" said Georges. "Still to add to the retirement fund!"

"As you say, Commandant, still to add to the retirement fund. You don't have any objection to my going to look for a little supplement to my pay?"

"None, my friend. But don't stay too long, or we'll be anxious."

"Oh, half an hour or three-quarters."

With that, Quosé departed, cheerfully humming a sea-shanty.

Scarcely ten minutes had gone by when precipitate footsteps sounded on the far side of the barrage of stalactites. Quosé was coming back at a run. The doctor, who was getting ready to attach a joist to the cable that Georges was extending to him, stopped. The Commandant, understanding instinctively that Halgouët would not be coming back at such a speed without a grave reason, came down from the top of the pylon in two seconds, with the agility typical of a mariner.

When the Breton appeared at the opening of the barrage his companions were alarmed by the distress of his features.

"What is it, Halgouët?" they demanded, in unison.

"It's…it's water! The sea, the inundation, that's following me, that's right behind me, that's going to reach us—and look!"

Indeed, behind Halgouët, a sheet of water was invading the corridor, passing over the stalagmites of lava welded to the rocky ground at the entrance to the cavern, and extending over the floor of the grotto in a large fan fringed with foam. In a matter of seconds, it was up to the mariners' ankles.

"Well," cried Georges, with his captain's coolness under pressure, "the water is the sea, and the sea we know, we mariners! Pull yourself together, Halgouët, and pay attention to the maneuver. Quickly, let's embark the tools, the food and the cables in the big sarcophagus, which will serve us as a canoe. Don't worry about the wood—it will float, and we can always recover it. This

196

inundation, my friends, will hasten the denouement. It's probably what will save us—but there's not a minute to lose!"

With a military precision, each one took charge of loading some object into the sarcophagus. Halgouët had recovered himself completely thanks to the assure energy of the Commandant. In less than three minutes he was able to shout: "All done!"

It was just in time. The water was still rising, without violence, but rapidly, as occurs in a reservoir filling up by the regular flow of a water-pipe. By the time the sarcophagus, floating like a watertight vessel on its broad, flat bottom, was completely equipped the three men were up to their hips in water, and they were obliged to take careful precautions not to capsize the skiff as they installed themselves within it.

Around them, on the lake thus formed, pieces of wood were floating like wreckage. As for the pylon, they had taken care when constructing it, as a safety measure to increase its solidity, to drive the four uprights that served as its edges a meter into the ground. The water, rising without any shock, almost without eddies, did not shake it.

"This is what we're going to do," said Georges. We don't know how far below sea level the floor of the cavern is. There are three possibilities: either the water will rise as far as the opening, and we'll be able to get out it naturally, once we're outside, by climbing up the volcanic cone; or it will stop below the level that we've reached with our tower, in which case, we'll collect these scattered spars and purely and simply continue our work; or, finally, it will stop above the construction—which is to say, bringing us within two or three meters of the opening—and in that case, we'll maintain ourselves underneath it, steering as best we can using joists as oars or gaffes, and we'll throw our two iron levers outside, attached as a cross and tied to a rope; if we don't succeed at the first attempt, it will be extraordinary is we don't manage, by repeated tries, in getting the improvised grapnel to catch of something eventually, and we'll be able to hoist ourselves up by the cable."

"Of course!" exclaimed Halgouët. "It's quite simple—only it was necessary to think of it all, and I confess that, for my part, I wouldn't have got there so quickly."

"You're right, my dear Georges," said Sergeant, "but I confess that I can't help being only partly reassured. In any logical reasoning formulated with the mathematical clarity that you've given to yours, there's a part to play for a neglected or unanticipated hypothesis."

"So be it," replied the Commandant. "If it presents itself, we'll face up to the danger it brings. In the meantime, let's act in accordance with what we know and start making our grapnel right away.

The operation was completed by Halgouët and Georges in a matter of minutes. The two levers were solidly bound together in the form of a cross, and they added to the system a wooden bar perpendicular to the plain of the cross, sharpened at both ends by means of Halgouët's knife. In that manner it would be difficult for the apparatus, thrown outside, not to bite, either in the soil, on a root or some crevice in the rock. They attached about ten meters of cable to the grapnel, fixing it by means of a solid knot to one of the flaps on the projections on the coffin, which marked the location of the shoulders. Then they collected a few floating spars, and waited.

Already, no more than a meter of the tower still protruded from the water. As they rose up within the grotto, they noticed that it widened out at the top, and the depths thus unmasked revealed dark corners into which the light did not penetrate.

The three men remained anxiously silent. Halgouët, at the prow—at the head, as he said, laughing—held on to one of the edges of the pylon, and guided the boat alongside the tower as the water continued to rise. The doctor with a spar in hand, got ready to paddle. Georges, at the rear, held the grapnel and tried to assume a vigorous stance from which to throw it.

Nothing troubled the silence reigning over the scene, except for the song of a little bird, which, free and intoxicated by sunlight and gaiety, was perched on one of the tamarisks that inclined over the edge of the grotto's mouth.

The water was still rising. Gradually, the extremities of the unfinished pylon sank into the calm invasive lake.

Suddenly a violent current was manifest at the surface of the water, thus far dormant. The improvised boat was subject to a sudden jolt, and pivoted on itself, Halgouët, clinging to the summit of one of the beams of the pylon, his arm shoulder-deep in the water, tried to hold on, but the wood broke and the Breton cut his hand trying to seize another piece of the frame in passing.

"Look, Commandant," said the doctor, standing up, his finger extended. "There it is—the neglected hypothesis. Look!"

Georges looked, and he saw, in one of the dark corners of the cavern, an even blacker patch, a rip in the wall, through which the water, surpassing its level, was precipitating as if into a drain, determining one of the terrible currents felt at the top of cataracts.

He did not lose his head. With a sure hand he threw the grapnel through the opening. The device caught immediately, outside. For a moment, the boat, thus anchored, stopped.

"Come on," my friends," said Georges. "Let's get out. Hoist yourselves up the cable—Halgouët first.!

"Commandant!"

"Obey!"

The matelot seized the rope, but just as he was about to pull himself up by his wrists, the violence of the current increased. The cable broke, and the boat, now irresistibly dragged away, was engulfed in a black tunnel so low that the three men had to crouch down in order not to break their heads on the rock that formed its vault.

They traveled this for a distance they were never able to determine. The blow that had struck them at the very moment when they thought their martyrdom was about to end was so unexpected, so shattering, that all three suffered a moment of absence, a minute of veritable madness and mental aberration. Silent and breathless, huddled together in the bottom of the skiff, they were scarcely able to take account of the moment when their vessel came to a stop. Plunged in darkness, deafened by the noise of the water that was precipitating them rapidly down the outflow through which it had found its route, dazed by that brutal and decisive defeat, they were no longer even thinking about attempting an effort, of trying some impossible means of salvation.

Those three men of heroic courage and superhuman composure, who had sustained for more than twenty days, almost without weakening, a gigantic struggle against an implacable fate, were vanquished, unable even to find a word of adieu for one another, or to communicate their final thought other than by a mute and instinctive pressure of the hands. They were like ancient gladiators, mortally wounded in the arena by a final adversary after having slain a dozen, lying on the floor of the circus, resigned, awaiting death and eternal repose.

Then, suddenly, at the very moment when despair covered their energy with its black veil; at the very moment when each of them, in the imminence of inevitable death, no longer retained in his almost-extinct intelligence anything but a vague and indecisive thought of dear ones lost forever; at the moment when, alone in that disarray of the heat and the brain, like a persistent glimmer, the aspiration subsisted of souls toward almighty God; at that supreme moment…they heard a distant and formidable thunderclap.

At the same time, the stone vault fractured a few meters ahead of them, an avalanche of rocks plunged into the water, leaving a gaping opening through which daylight penetrated again, and on the edges of which, by virtue of the slope of the vault, the torrent that was carrying them away had just broken. Their skiff, caught sideways, was braced against the two walls.

By virtue of a mechanical movement, still almost unconscious in the shadow of the tomb that they had seen open up, they threw themselves into the water and swam.

X
Resurrection

It will be remembered that Sir Owen had been very surprised to see that Madame de Malher, pursued by her obsession that her husband was not dead, had nevertheless consented to choose the place on the islet of Syrtos where the monument to the victims of the Syrtos was to be erected.

The following day, in fact, Madame de Malher was the first to ask when they were going to land. Sir Owen replied that he could have a launch equipped as soon as the *Sirius* had departed for Piraeus.

In conformity with the orders he had given, everything had been prepared during the night for setting sail. One of the steamers was to take the refloated ship directly in tow. The other, linked to the *Sirius* by a mooring-rope, was to escort the convoy, ready to intervene in case any accident, or the impact of a big wave overloaded the tow-rope and broke it.

The captain of the *Investigator* had embarked a number of his own crewmen aboard the Sirius, charged with keeping watch to see that no further damage was sustained en route. By virtue of a delicate thought, he did not want the French ship to arrive in Piraeus manned by a exclusively English crew, and asked the French engineer who had assisted him to take command of his men—which would offer the advantage of enabling the initiation a competent individual to intervene immediately if any unexpected incident did occur.

Sir Owen would have liked Poulpiquet and the divers to embark as well, but Halgouët's friend asked on his own behalf and that of his companions, as a supreme recompense for their communal effort, to participate in the construction of the funereal monument, in order that French hands might be associated with that final homage. As the time-limit stipulated by Admiral de la Rénolière when placing his mariners at Sir Owen's disposition had not yet been reached, the captain of the Investigator granted the worthy men's request.

At nine o'clock, al the preparations were complete. The Greek steamers, under pressure, were only waiting for the signal to depart. Sir Owen went aboard the *Sirius* and made a tour of the unfortunate vessel. The appearance of the deck was almost normal, all the more so as the yacht's sailors had striven to mask, by means of ingenious artifice, the damage caused by the wreck, but the interior presented a lamentable spectacle. The carpets of the cabins and stair-heads were discolored, their bright colors faded into a neutral dullness; the instruments of navigation, barometers lamps and handrails, which had once, maintained with scrupulous solicitude, shone like gold, were covered with a green layer of copper oxide. The mahogany of the tables and the woodwork, once polished like mirrors, was warped, water-stained and split, exposing the fibers of the wood. The floor was strewn with a multitude of disparate objects: table or kitchen utensils, toilet necessities, items of clothing, rusty weapons, and swollen books with the pages stuck together.

In the Commandant's cabin, the wall against which the strong-box containing the ship's papers and treasury had been sealed had given way, and the iron cupboard was leaning, supported by the frame of the bunk. Sir

Owen collected a few objects from that chamber: two frames containing corroded photographs, a saber, a watch and a pocket-knife—souvenirs that he intended to give to his niece.

The engine appeared, between the broken partitions, like an immense yellowing skeleton under the thick layer of rust that had invaded it. In the crew quarters and between decks there was an inextricable tangle of hammocks, mattresses and blankets, mingled pell-mell with rifles, hatchets, sabers, mess-tins, pans and clothes-chests.

Once the tour was concluded, Sir Owen posted two sentries before the Commandant's safe, which would only be opened in the presence of the French consul, went back on deck, and gave the order to set forth from the height of the bridge. The towing cable tautened, and, encumbered by the girdle of floats that surrounded her, hesitantly, as if surprised to be cleaving the waves again after having slept the deep slumber of lost ships under the sea, the *Sirius* slowly began to move.

Then Sir Owen handed the flag that he had brought within him to one of the sailors. The man mounted it on the flagstaff, and, on the *Sirius* as aboard the Geek ships and the Investigator, everyone bared their heads while the tricolor rose up the mast of the ship that France was about to recover.

A few minutes later, having acquired the certainty that the navigation could proceed in adequate conditions, Sir Owen shook the engineer's hand one last time, descended into the launch and returned to his own ship.

As he came back he crossed the path of a boar that was taking a crew ashore who would undertake the initial excavations once the location of the monument had been determined; it comprised three English mariners and the French divers, who wanted the honor of delivering the first blows of the pickax.

An hour later, Madame de Malher disembarked, in the company of her uncle, on the islet of Syrtos.

It was impossible to imagine a landscape more desolate than that island, which was less than two kilometers in circumference. The bare rock plunged directly into the sea, and it was with difficulty that they discovered a little inlet where the launches could run aground on a minuscule sandy beach. Everywhere, all the way to the foot of the volcanic cone, over which light smoke drifted at times, the ground was covered with a kind of clay, cracked by the alternate action of rain and sun, evidently originating from volcanic ash of a particular nature: the same clay that had deposited a waterproof layer over the carapace of the dead city. As far as the eye could see, there was no trace of vegetation except for a few meager tamarisks, pink heather and two or three wild fig-trees, which were growing in the sparse accumulations of fertile soil brought by storms.

Sir Owen proposed to erect the monument half way up the cone, on a kind of rocky platform, which was visible from a long way off—but Madame Malher did not share that opinion.

"If my husband and his companions really have perished," she said, "it's the sea that is their sepulcher. And since the monument that we shall erect to them is also a tomb, I want it to be placed as close as possible to the place where they lie. I'd therefore like it to be erected close to the shore. The mariners skirting the coast of Syrtos will thus see it more distinctly. It will be easier for those passing by at sea to learn to whose memory it has been erected; it will be easier to read, on coming ashore, the inscription that they would perhaps be reluctant to go half way up the mountain to decipher—and as the brave mariners that pass near this point of desolation won't fail to address a prayer to Heaven, they will be able to include a name in it!"

Sir Owen yielded. They chose a kind of excrescence of the ground, a low-set hillock situated a few meters from the shore, close enough to satisfy Madame de Malher's desire but far enough away for the monument to be sheltered from degradation by the sea on stormy days. The decision made, Sir Owen had the square traced out where the foundations would be dug. Poulpiquet made the sign of the cross, picked up his pickax, and delivered the first blow. His companions also attacked the ground

After a few minutes, however, they were obliged to stop. The clay was only ten centimeters thick. Beneath it, they were attacking a hard and resistant layer of lava.

"Commandant," said Poulpiquet, our tools are chipping on that rock. My opinion is that we'll have to employ a mine."

"You're right, my friend," Sir Owen replied. "I'll send someone to fetch cartridges." Then he turned to his niece. "My poor child," he said, "you have nothing to do for the moment. Your wish has been granted; let's allow these worthy men to work and go back aboard."

The young woman took her uncle's arm. She went down as far as the little beach. Then, before embarking in the launch, like a desolate widow who cannot resign herself to leave a grave that is still open, she put her hands together, and with an almost supplicant voice, she asked her uncle for permission to stay.

In vain, Sir Owen told her that she needed rest and to conserve her strength, that the sun was hot and that there was no shelter. Nothing worked. She was obstinate, still gentle but form, and for fear of provoking a crisis, Sir Owen was obliged to give in.

They brought the cover from one of the boats, made a seat with the cushions from the stern, and the young woman installed herself beneath an improvised tent, her hands clasped and her eyes fixed on the group of French and English mariners,, who, at rest, leaning on their picks, were waiting for the return of the boat that had gone o fetch cartridges from aboard the *Investigator*.

The mine was soon set up. When the fuse was ready, everyone retreated a hundred meters. One of the yacht's crewmen, who combined the duties of helmsman with functions of gunner and pyrotechnist, lit the fuse and came rapidly to join the group formed by the laborers and spectators.

A minute went by.

Suddenly, there was jet of fire. A muffled detonation was heard, reverberated like a thunderclap by the echoes of the mountain. At the same time, a spray of stone fragments was hurled into the air; a large hole opened up at the location of the mine, and to the profound stupefaction of the witnesses, a column of water sprang from the opening, chased by the soaring blocks of stone.

Everyone ran toward the hole to discover the cause of that strange phenomenon, but as they arrived half way, the sailors and Sir Owen stopped dead, nailed to the spot, startled and almost terrified, while Madame de Malher fell to her knees.

From the hole providentially opened by the mine, three men emerged, emaciated and clad in rags, streaming with water, hoisting themselves out with difficulty, and standing up, haggard and bewildered, not daring to

believe, as yet, in their improbable salvation, their resurrection.

They were the three missing men of the *Sirius*.

X
Conclusion

Of what happened at that moment we shall say nothing. There are joys whose frightful intensity no pen can render.

By a miracle due to the youth and robust constitution of our heroes, the latter supported the joy as they had endured the insults of fate.

An hour later, reunited in the saloon of the *Investigator*, with the valiant wife beside her husband, fortified by the cares that were lavished upon then, they sketched an account of their terrible adventures. And while they spoke, the mariners of the *Investigator*, in spite of discipline, and in spite of their ignorance of the French language, gathered around the doors of the yacht's saloon, seeking to grasp and divine a few scraps of their strange narrative.

Our role as faithful narrator ends here. It only remains to say what became of the three missing men of the *Sirius* and their friends.

In spite of that terrible episode, Georges de Malher did not abandon his naval career. He is due to be appointed as the captain of a frigate imminently. After taking six months of leave that were certainly owed to him, he has asked permission from the Ministry of Marine to devote two years to the execution of a plan formulated by Sir Owen.

The latter, has, in fact, been possessed by an idea that is the consequence of the drama in which he was involved. He had given himself the task of avoiding collisions at sea, and has undertaken, as a commencement, to rid the major Atlantic sea-lanes of numerous wrecks that constitute a terrible and permanent danger to navigation.

Jean Halgouët, alias Quosé, had requested a convalescent leave that will take him to the end of his term of service. He has returned to his little Breton village and, thanks to the ingots of Egyptian gold, has bought a comfortable fishing-boat which he had baptized the *Momie*, which amazed his neighbors. At first they thought he was mad, until the day when a syndicate of seamen, having obtained information, declared solemnly that "according to what the Ministry had written to them," the adventures he recounted were accurate.

His friend Poulpiquet has come to join him, and will serve as his mate. They both received the military medal on the first of January last year.

As for the doctor, his first concern, on arriving at Piraeus, was to make his preparations to go and study cholera in Beyrouth. He learned to his great annoyance that the epidemic had suddenly come to an end after a week.

"Damn!" he said, in a bad temper. "It's decidedly written that I shall never see cholera."

All three men, linked together by such terrible ordeals and such poignant memories, have remained in continual correspondence with one another. It is at their common expense that they wanted to erect a monument on the islet, which only bears a single name: that of the young midshipman who died doing his duty. Dispersed for the moment, they write long letters to one another, which all terminate with the wish to meet again in less terrible circumstances.

Their wishes are to be granted, and we shall find those brave men again, grouped around Sir Owen in his endeavor of humanity and courage.

SF & FANTASY

Adolphe Alhaiza. *Cybele*

Alphonse Allais. *The Adventures of Captain Cap*

Henri Allorge. *The Great Cataclysm*

Guy d'Armen. *Doc Ardan: The City of Gold and Lepers*

G.-J. Arnaud. *The Ice Company*

Charles Asselineau. *The Double Life*

Henri Austruy. *The Eupantophone; The Olotelepan; The Petitpaon Era*

Barillet-Lagargousse. *The Final War*

Cyprien Bérard. *The Vampire Lord Ruthwen*

S. Henry Berthoud. *Martyrs of Science*

Aloysius Bertrand. *Gaspard de la Nuit*

Richard Bessière. *The Gardens of the Apocalypse; The Masters of Silence*

Albert Bleunard. *Ever SMalher*

Félix Bodin. *The Novel of the Future*

Louis Boussenard. *Monsieur Synthesis*

Alphonse Brown. *City of Glass; The Conquest of the Air*

Emile Calvet. *In a Thousand Years*

André Caroff. *The Terror of Madame Atomos; Miss Atomos; The Return of Madame Atomos; The Mistake of Madame Atomos; The Monsters of Madame Atomos; The Revenge of Madame Atomos; The Resurrection of Madame Atomos; The Mark of Madame Atomos; The Spheres of Madame Atomos; The Wrath of Madame Atomos* (w/M. & Sylvie Stéphan)

Félicien Champsaur. *The Human Arrow; Ouha, King of the Apes; Pharaoh's Wife; Homo-Deus*

Didier de Chousy. *Ignis*

Jules Clarétie. *Obsession*

Michel Corday. *The Eternal Flame*

André Couvreur. *The Necessary Evil*; *Caresco, Superman; The Exploits of Professor Tornada* (3 vols.)

Captain Danrit. *Undersea Odyssey*

C. I. Defontenay. *Star (Psi Cassiopeia)*

Charles Derennes. *The People of the Pole*

Georges Dodds (anthologist). *The Missing Link*

Charles Dodeman. *The Silent Bomb*

Harry Dickson. *The Heir of Dracula; Harry Dickson vs. The Spider*

Georges Le Faure & Henri de Graffigny. *The Extraordinary Adventures of a Russian Scientist Across the Solar System* (2 vols.)
Gustave Le Rouge. *The Mysterious Doctor Cornelius* (3 vols.); *The Vampires of Mars; The Dominion of the World* (w/Gustave Guitton) (4 vols.)
Jules Lermina. *Mysteryville; Panic in Paris; To-Ho and the Gold Destroyers; The Secret of Zippeliu; The Battle of Strasbourg*
André Lichtenberger. *The Centaurs; The Children of the Crab*
Listonai. *The Philosophical Voyager*
Jean-Marc & Randy Lofficier. *Edgar Allan Poe on Mars; The Katrina Protocol; Pacifica; Robonocchio; Return of the Nyctalope;* (anthologists) *Tales of the Shadowmen 1-11; The Vampire Almanac*
Xavier Mauméjean. *The League of Heroes*
Joseph Méry. *The Tower of Destiny*
Hippolyte Mettais. *The Year 5865; Paris Before the Deluge*
Louise Michel. *The Human Microbes; The New World*
Tony Moilin. *Paris in the Year 2000*
José Moselli. *Illa's End*
John-Antoine Nau. *Enemy Force*
Marie Nizet. *Captain Vampire*
C. Nodier, A. Beraud & Toussaint-Merle. *Frankenstein*
Henri de Parville. *An Inhabitant of the Planet Mars*
Gaston de Pawlowski. *Journey to the Land of the 4th Dimension*
Georges Pellerin. *The World in 2000 Years*
Ernest Pérochon. *The Frenetic People*
Pierre Pelot. *The Child Who Walked on the Sky*
J. Polidori, C. Nodier, E. Scribe. *Lord Ruthven the Vampire*
P.-A. Ponson du Terrail. *The Vampire and the Devil's Son; The Immortal Woman*
Edgar Quinet. *Ahasuerus; The Enchanter Merlin*
Henri de Régnier. *A Surfeit of Mirrors*
Maurice Renard. *The Blue Peril; Doctor Lerne; The Doctored Man; A Man Among the Microbes; The Master of Light*
Jean Richepin. *The Wing; The Crazy Corner*
Albert Robida. *The Adventures of Saturnin Farandoul; The Clock of the Centuries; Chalet in the Sky; The Electric Life*
J.-H. Rosny Aîné. *Helgvor of the Blue River; The Givreuse Enigma; The Mysterious Force; The Navigators of Space; Vamireh; The World of the Variants; The Young Vampire*
Marcel Rouff. *Journey to the Inverted World*
Léonie Rouzade. *The World Turned Upside Down*

Han Ryner. *The Superhumans; The Human Ant*
Pierre de Selenes: *An Unknown World*
Angelo de Sorr. *The Vampires of London*
Brian Stableford. *The New Faust at the Tragicomique;The Empire of the Necromancers (The Shadow of Frankenstein; Frankenstein and the Vampire Countess; Frankenstein in London); Sherlock Holmes & The Vampires of Eternity; The Stones of Camelot; The Wayward Muse.* (anthologist) *News from the Moon; The Germans on Venus; The Supreme Progress; The World Above the World; Nemoville; Investigations of the Future; The Conqueror of Death; The Revolt of the Machines*
Jacques Spitz. *The Eye of Purgatory*
Kurt Steiner. *Ortog*
Eugène Thébault. *Radio-Terror*
C.-F. Tiphaigne de La Roche. *Amilec*
Simon Tyssot de Patot. *The Strange Voyages of Jacques Massé and Pierre de Mésange*
Louis Ulbach. *Prince Bonifacio*
Théo Varlet. *The Golden Rock. The Xenobiotic Invasion; The Castaways of Eros; Timeslip Troopers* (w/André Blandin); *The Martian Epic* (w/Octave Joncquel)
Pierre Véron. *The Merchants of Health*
Paul Vibert. *The Mysterious Fluid*
Villiers de l'Isle-Adam. *The Scaffold; The Vampire Soul*
Philippe Ward. *Artahe ; The Song of Montségur* (w/Sylvie Miller) *Manhattan Ghost* (w/Mickael Laguerre)

MYSTERIES & THRILLERS

M. Allain & P. Souvestre. *The Daughter of Fantômas*
A. Anicet-Bourgeois, Lucien Dabril. *Rocambole*
A. Bernède. *Belphegor; Judex* (w/Louis Feuillade); *The Return of Judex* (w/Louis Feuillade); *The Shadow of Judex*
A. Bisson & G. Livet. *Nick Carter vs. Fantômas*
V. Darlay & H. de Gorsse. *Arsène Lupin vs. Sherlock Holmes: The Stage Play*
Séamas Duffy. *Sherlock Holmes in Paris*
Paul Féval. *Gentlemen of the Night; John Devil; The Black Coats ('Salem Street; The Invisible Weapon; The Parisian Jungle; The Companions of the Treasure; Heart of Steel; The Cadet Gang; The Sword-Swallower)*

Emile Gaboriau. *Monsieur Lecoq*

Goron & Emile Gautier. *Spawn of the Penitentiary*

Paul d'Ivoi. *Around the World on Five Sous* (w/Henri Chabrillat)

Rick Lai. *Shadows of the Opera: Retribution in Blood; Sisters of the Shadows: The Curse of Cagliostro*

Steve Leadley. *Sherlock Holmes: The Circle of Blood*

Maurice Leblanc. *Arsène Lupin vs. Countess Cagliostro; Arsène Lupin vs. Sherlock Holmes (The Blonde Phantom; The Hollow Needle); The Many Faces of Arsène Lupin; The Island of the Thirty Coffins*

Gaston Leroux. *Chéri-Bibi; The Phantom of the Opera; Rouletabille & the Mystery of the Yellow Room; Rouletabille at Krupp's*

Richard Marsh. *The Complete Adventures of Judith Lee*

William Patrick Maynard. *The Terror of Fu Manchu; The Destiny of Fu Manchu*

Frank J. Morlock. *Sherlock Holmes: The Grand Horizontals; Sherlock Holmes vs Jack the Ripper*

Jean Petithuguenin. *The Adventures of Ethel King*

Antonin Reschal. *The Adventures of Miss Boston*

P. de Wattyne & Y. Walter. *Sherlock Holmes vs. Fantômas*

David White. *Fantômas in America*

Pierre Yrondy. *The Adventures of Thérèse Arnaud*

Victor Margueritte. *The Bacheloress; The Companion; The Couple*

SCREENPLAYS

Mike Baron. *The Iron Triangle*

Emma Bull & Will Shetterly. *Nightspeeder; War for the Oaks*

Gerry Conway & Roy Thomas. *Doc Dynamo*

Steve Englehart. *Majorca*

James Hudnall. *The Devastator*

Jean-Marc & Randy Lofficier. *Royal Flush*

J.-M. & R. Lofficier & Marc Agapit. *Despair*

J.-M. & R. Lofficier & Joël Houssin. *City*

Andrew Paquette. *Peripheral Vision*

Robert L. Robinson, Jr. *Judex*

R. Thomas, J. Hendler & L. Sprague de Camp. *Rivers of Time*

NON-FICTION

Stephen R. Bissette. *Blur 1-5. Green Mountain Cinema 1; Teen Angels*
Win Scott Eckert. *Crossovers* (2 vols.)
Jean-Marc & Randy Lofficier. *Shadowmen* (2 vols.)
Randy Lofficier. *Over Here*

ART BOOKS

Jean-Pierre Normand. *Science Fiction Illustrations*
Raven Okeefe. *Raven's L'il Critters; Rave's Faves*
Randy Lofficier & Raven Okeefe. *If Your Possum Go Daylight...*
Daniele Serra. *Illusions*
Randy Lofficier. *Over Here*

HEXAGON COMICS

Franco Frescura & Luciano Bernasconi. *Wampus*
Franco Frescura & Giorgio Trevisan. *CLASH*
L. Bernasconi, J.-M. Lofficier & Juan Roncagliolo. *Phenix*
Claude Legrand, J.-M. Lofficier & L. Bernasconi. *Kabur*
Franco Oneta. *Zembla*
L. Buffolente, Lofficier & J.-J. Dzialowski. *Strangers: Homicron*
Danilo Grossi. *Strangers: Jaydee*
Claude Legrand & Luciano Bernasconi. *Strangers: Starlock*
Thierry Mornet & Juan Roncagliolo. *Guardian of the Republic*
J.-M. Lofficier, M. Garcia, F. Blanco & J. Pima. *Strangers in a Strange Land*